## "My fiancé doesn't like you," Caitlin stated flatly

"The feeling is mutual," Rogan bit out. "I wonder why that is?"

She turned away. "I have no idea."

"Don't you?" Rogan taunted.

Her face became flushed. "Please don't make trouble for me."

"Oh, I don't intend making trouble for you, Caity," drawled the American whom they called the Rogue.

"No?" she said.

"No," he confirmed calmly, "and I'm sure that in the end you'll make the only decision you can in the circumstances."

Caitlin frowned. "There's no decision to make. I'm going to marry Graham on Saturday."

Dark brows rose over mocking eyes. "Why, when you'll be unfaithful to him within a couple of months?"

"How dare you! You arrogant—" But her words were cut off by the assault of his mouth on hers.

Dear Reader,

This month we celebrate the publication of our 1000th Harlequin Presents. It is a special occasion for us, and one we would like to share with you.

Since its inception with three of our bestselling authors in May, 1973, Harlequin Presents has grown to become the most popular romance series in the world, featuring more than sixty internationally acclaimed authors. All of the authors appearing this month are well-known and loved. Some have been with us right from the start; others are newer, but each, in the tradition of Harlequin Presents, delivers the passionate exciting love stories our readers have come to expect.

We are proud of the trust you have placed in us over the years. It's part of the Harlequin dedication to supplying, contemporary fiction, rich in romance, exotic settings and happy endings.

We know you'll enjoy all of the selections in this very special month, and in the months to come.

Your friends at Harlequin

# CAROLE MORTIMER

a rogue and a pirate

**Harlequin Books**

TORONTO • NEW YORK • LONDON
AMSTERDAM • PARIS • SYDNEY • HAMBURG
STOCKHOLM • ATHENS • TOKYO • MILAN

For John,
Matthew and Joshua

Harlequin Presents first edition August 1987
ISBN 0-373-11005-7

Original hardcover edition published in 1986
by Mills & Boon Limited

# CHAPTER ONE

'MIND if I join you?'

Caitlin blinked up at the man who stood next to her, eyes the colour of sapphires flashing as brilliantly as the stone they resembled.

She had seen the man enter the lounge of this exclusive hotel; who hadn't noticed him as he hesitated in the doorway, surveying the occupants of the room with an arrogance that bordered on insolence, startlingly green eyes narrowed as he glanced around for somewhere to sit, all the seats at the bar being occupied?

She had absently acknowledged his attraction, the swathe of dark hair that fell rakishly across his forehead, brows the same colour jutting over eyes of luminous green, a long straight nose, and a hard slash of a mouth, its cynical twist softened by the fullness of the lower lip, his jaw firm and uncompromising. But it was his sheer size that had instantly drawn her attention, easily six foot four, maybe even slightly taller than that, his shoulders wide and powerful, tapering to narrow hips and thighs, his legs long and muscular in the fitted black denims he wore with such ease. It may even have been that casualness of appearance that had drawn her gaze in a room full of people dressed for dinner, the black shirt unbuttoned at the throat and the

7

tight denims standing out noticeably among the formal elegance.

After that initial dismissive perusal she had turned away. She hadn't expected him to choose her table as the one he wanted to sit at! But as she and the blonde woman sitting at the bar were the only unaccompanied females here, the latter having a man sitting either side of her, perhaps it wasn't so surprising that this man had chosen this table after all!

Caitlin gave an agreeable inclination of her head, the silky curtain of her flaming-red hair falling forward to touch her breasts as she did so. 'I was just about to leave anyway.' She picked up her clutch-bag.

Lean fingers encircled her wrist, the grip light but steely. 'Don't let me drive you away,' he urged, his accent on closer inspection definitely from across the Atlantic.

And he was close, surprisingly so, had chosen to sit in the chair next to hers rather than across from her. From a distance, his body lithe and lean, he had looked to be in his early thirties, but close to, the lines of cynicism were etched beside his eyes and mouth, putting him a little older than that, maybe thirty-five or thirty-six. There was an air of bored calculation about him, as if her answer was never in doubt, her reluctance only perfunctory.

Caitlin pointedly removed her arm from his grip. 'As I said, I was about to leave,' she bit out coldly.

Green eyes warmed at her icy manner, relaxing back in his chair, his long legs spread wide to accommodate their length beneath the low table. 'And leave a visiting American all alone?' he drawled mockingly.

Her brows rose coolly. 'I'm sure it doesn't have to be that way,' she dismissed uninterestedly.

'That was exactly what I thought when I saw *you* sitting here all alone,' he taunted, not at all ruffled by her haughty reply.

She drew in an angry breath. '*I* did happen to be alone through choice,' she snapped.

' "Misery loves company" ' he shrugged.

'I am not miserable, Mr——?' She quirked dark brows enquiringly.

'McCord—Rogan McCord,' he supplied lightly, his mouth still twisted into that patronising smile.

'Mr McCord,' she repeated abruptly. Rogan? What an unusual name! But somehow it suited him. 'I am perfectly happy, Mr McCord,' she bit out. 'Ecstatic, in fact,' she added tautly.

'Then why are you sitting all alone in a bar drinking?' he derided.

Caitlin sighed, wishing she had followed her first instinct and left while she had the chance. She should never have allowed herself to be drawn into conversation with this infuriating man! 'Because drinking is what you do in bars,' she told him caustically.

Rogan McCord shook his head. 'Not women on their own. And especially not women like you.'

She couldn't help herself, she rose to the bait he had deliberately set. 'A woman like me?'

He looked her over consideringly. 'Rich—I can

tell that by your designer-label gown,' he drawled mockingly, the warmth of his gaze telling her he approved of the shimmering petrol-blue gown, and the way it clung lovingly to her slender curves. 'And, of course, your public-school accent,' he added derisively. 'And you're uncomfortable being here, I could tell that by the way you kept looking around you.'

'How observant of you!' Her eyes flashed.

He shrugged. 'Was I right?'

'But of course,' she dismissed in a bored voice. 'Aren't you always?'

He grinned at her condescension, looking more rakish than ever. Unaccountably the image of the pirate heroes from the books she used to sneak out to buy while at boarding-school came to Caitlin's mind. She could just picture him aboard a pirate ship, lord of all he surveyed!

But she was no longer an impressionable fifteen, and six years on from those romantic dreams she used to weave in her head she realised there was nothing in the least romantic about this man, that he was just hoping to find a warm and willing woman to share his bed for the night. She was neither warm nor willing!

'For your information, Mr McCord,' she bit out impatiently, 'I was waiting for a friend who has obviously been delayed.'

'His loss is my gain.' He still smiled the confident smile of a seasoned flirt.

'I don't think so, Mr McCord,' she said drily. 'My friend was a she.' And Gayle should have been here half an hour ago, she thought irritably. She hadn't felt in the mood for driving into town in the first place, but Gayle had insisted. And now she had obviously let her down.

Rogan McCord sat forward with a sudden burst of energy that had been totally unexpected, having looked like a sleepy feline until that moment. 'Let me buy you a drink,' he suggested huskily.

Caitlin found herself a little unnerved by his sudden intensity. 'I already have one.' She indicated the drink in front of her that she had barely sipped before his intrusion into her solitude.

'All the more reason to stay a while longer and finish it,' he said triumphantly.

She moistened lips glossed a tempting red, her other make-up kept to the minimum, a light blue shadow on her lids, mascara lengthening the darkness of her lashes, blusher accentuating her high cheekbones beneath those slightly slanting eyes. She had been taught from an early age to make the best of her looks, knew exactly how to draw attention from her small snub of a nose, that tended to freckle during the summer months, so that it was the deep blue of her eyes that drew the admiration. Slightly above average height, she was willowy rather than curvaceous, her figure very suited to the fashions the Princess of Wales had made so popular.

But if her wealthy background had taught her how to put on make-up, and allowed her to dress well, it had also shown her how to give a practised flirt a set-down! 'I have no wish to finish anything with you except this conversation,' she snapped.

He rose politely to his feet as she stood up to leave. 'It's been nice meeting you, Miss——?' He deliberately aped her way of finding out his name.

'O'Rourke,' she supplied tersely. 'Caitlin O'Rourke.'

'Irish?' he derided.

'What do you think?' Her eyes flashed.

'I think that with your Irish ancestry and my Scottish one sparks were sure to fly,' he drawled, his eyes brimming with laughter. 'They began to do that for me the moment I looked at you,' he added drily. 'You're very beautiful, Caitlin O'Rourke.'

'Thank you.' She was unimpressed by the compliment.

His mouth quirked. 'You've heard it all before, hm?' he said self-derisively.

'Or something like it.' She gave a haughty inclination of her head. 'Insincere flattery to get a woman into bed is as old as time!'

'But it wasn't insincere,' he drawled. 'You really are lovely, Caity O'Rourke.'

Her cheeks flamed. 'My name is Caitlin.' Only her family ever used that affectionate shortening of her given name.

'Of course it is,' he humoured. 'But I'm sure that when a man makes love to you he calls you Caity.'

'How dare you, you—you *pirate*, you!' She was breathing heavily in her agitation, at once mortified at the lapse in temper that had made her blurt out her secret opinion of him so bluntly.

Rogan grinned, his brows raised. 'So that's how I

appear to you, is it?' he speculated. 'Caitlin O'Rourke, you surprise me!'

She surprised herself. She was twenty-one years old, had stopped reading those swashbuckling novels years ago, and yet one look at Rogan McCord and they all came flooding back to her as he epitomised every fantasy she had ever had of a dark, arrogant pirate invading her life. But this was the twentieth century, for goodness' sake!

She drew herself frostily up to her full height. 'I'm sure I'm not the first woman to view your—persistence in that light.'

'You're the first one to ever say it to my face. I think I like it,' he smiled. 'Unless,' he sobered, 'you were thinking of Bluebeard? I can assure you I'm not married,' he derided, frowning as she seemed to pale. 'Are you?' He watched her closely. 'Because if you're a bored little socialite wife looking for some excitement in your life by taking a lover I think I should tell you you're doing this all wrong; you're supposed to encourage me, not push me away!'

'You don't seem to need any encouraging!' Her eyes flashed.

'True,' Rogan drawled. 'But then that should save us a lot of time.'

'Mr McCord,' she rasped, 'I am not married, neither am I looking for any more excitement in my life.'

'None of us can have too much excitement in our lives,' he drawled.

'In your case that's probably true,' she said scathingly, sure this man liked to experience anything made available to him. But *she* wasn't available! 'But I am not on the lookout for some brief meaningless affair.'

'You aren't giving us a chance,' he taunted. 'Our affair might not be brief or meaningless.'

'It would be meaningless because we don't even know each other, and it would be brief because I'm sure you don't intend to remain long in this country.'

Rogan shrugged. 'I could change my plans.'

'We aren't going to have an affair,' she told him agitatedly.

'Why not? I'd like nothing better than to take you to bed right now.'

She gave him a dazed frown. 'Mr McCord, are you usually this—blunt?'

He shrugged. 'Not always, no,' he answered consideringly.

'Then please don't make me the exception,' Caitlin snapped.

One lean hand moved up to caress her cheek with his knuckles. 'But I'd like to,' he murmured throatily.

She moved her head back from that caress, her hair moving in a shimmering red curtain. 'I have to go,' she said abruptly. 'It was—an experience, meeting you,' she added derisively.

He gave a regretful grimace for her determination to leave. 'You too.'

She could feel him watching her as she walked to the doorway, a tingle of awareness down her spine, telling herself she mustn't look back, that she shouldn't give him that satisfaction.

It was a compulsion, instinct, and she paused in the doorway to turn and look at Rogan McCord one last time.

He had been joined by the tiny blonde woman with the voluptuous curves who had been sitting alone at the bar!

The two of them were chatting amiably, Rogan ordering them a drink, his attention turning to Caitlin as he saw her standing in the doorway watching them. He gave her a mocking acknowledgement with his head, laughter in his eyes as Caitlin gave him a fierce glare before turning away.

He must have waited all of ten seconds after her departure before inviting the voluptuous blonde to join him!

She was still fuming at his high-handed conceit when she swung into the low Mercedes, her clutch-bag landing with a thud on the seat beside her. Who did he think he was, trying to pick her up in that way! No man had *ever* tried to pick her up in a bar before. Or so nearly succeeded!

There had been something about Mr Rogan McCord that was extremely appealing, his rakish charm a challenge, his almost casual confidence in his own attraction doubly so.

But he was also a rake and a flirt, out for a good time with the first woman he felt attracted to.

Or the second! Ten seconds, that was all he had waited before turning his attention to the blonde.

By the time she had finished berating Rogan McCord's rakish behaviour she had also realised that her car wasn't going to start.

Damn! Hopeless with anything mechanical, she knew there wasn't even any point in her looking under the bonnet; it all looked like a mess of wires and nuts to her. She was going to have to call someone out from the garage the family used to service their cars, wait for them to arrive, and then hope that it wasn't anything too serious. And all because Gayle had thought it would be a good idea if they had a drink together tonight. She had called Gayle a friend to Rogan McCord, but that wasn't quite true, and she now blamed the other woman for dragging her into town in the first place, especially as she hadn't even had the decency to turn up.

'Having trouble?' drawled an infuriatingly familiar voice.

Caught standing outside her car, telling it what a useless piece of junk it was, by Rogan McCord, she rounded on him sharply. 'No, I always talk to my car before driving it,' she snapped, turning to walk back in the direction of the hotel.

'Really?' he fell into step beside her. 'Is that a little like talking to plants?'

She gave his innocently enquiring face a scathing look, ignoring him as she located the public telephones in the reception area, turning her back on him as she dialled the number of the garage. The call went straight through to the mechanic on call, and she impatiently answered his queries with an obvious lack of knowledge about anything concerning cars except how to drive one. The man promised to come out immediately.

Caitlin came to a halt as she turned and almost bumped into the man leaning on the wall behind her, his arms folded across his chest, his expression gently mocking. 'Excuse me,' she bit out, pointedly moving past him to the lounge area beside the reception desks where she had told the mechanic she would be waiting for him.

'I can see how you would have to talk to your car before attempting to drive it.' Rogan McCord folded his lean length down into the low beige leather armchair opposite hers. 'You have a decided lack of respect for their delicate engineering!'

She looked across at him with frosty blue eyes. 'I don't remember asking you to join me.'

'Neither do I,' he answered cheerfully. 'But I've decided to overlook your lack of manners this time.'

Her mouth firmed. 'And I suppose you think it was *polite* to eavesdrop on my telephone call!'

He shrugged broad shoulders. 'I was waiting to use the telephone.'

'Then why didn't you?' Her eyes flashed.

'I changed my mind,' he dismissed tauntingly, eyeing her flushed face with amusement.

Caitlin gave a disbelieving snort before turning to watch the automatic doors for the arrival of the mechanic. She knew it was too soon for him to arrive yet, but anything was better than looking at Rogan McCord! Why wasn't he still with the blonde? Maybe she had turned him down too, Caitlin thought with satisfaction.

'I pity the poor devil at the receiving end of that smile,' he murmured, his eyes narrowed.

She looked at him with cool blue eyes. 'Self-pity is so boring, don't you think?'

He grinned, those deep slashes grooved into the hardness of his cheeks. 'Plotting my downfall, were you?' he drawled.

'To tell you the truth, Mr McCord, I don't care if I never have to think of you again,' she told him in a bored voice. 'I was just musing over your luck in choosing the wrong woman twice in one night.'

Dark brows rose over sea-green eyes. 'I didn't choose you at all, Caity, you were just there.'

'My name is Caitlin,' she snapped. 'And I was there because I was meeting someone.'

'Who didn't turn up,' he added derisively.

'It does happen,' she insisted defensively.

He shook his head. 'Not to women like you.'

'I wish you would stop saying that!' She glared. 'And I am not in the habit of sitting around in bars alone!'

'Of course you aren't,' Rogan humoured her.

Her eyes shot sparks of blue fire at him. 'Unlike your next choice,' she said bitchily.

'How could I even see another woman after you?' he taunted. 'Miranda was the one to approach me.'

Caitlin's scathing retort didn't pass her lips, her attention distracted by the woman under discussion as she walked past them to the doors in the company of a tall sandy-haired man, the look she shot Rogan wistful to say the least.

Caitlin turned to the man opposite her with new eyes. He didn't look as if having a woman approach *him* was a new experience, rather an accepted one, and to a woman who had never been the one to make the first move with any man it was totally unacceptable to her personal code of behaviour. No matter how attractive she found a man she could never be the first one to show that.

'Don't look so surprised,' Rogan derided at her silence. 'Miranda is a professional.'

'I don't—— *What?*' Her gasped exclamation couldn't be halted, even though she knew how young and naïve it made her seem. A prostitute? Here?

Rogan's mouth twisted in enjoyment of her disbelief. 'They have to ply their wares somewhere,' he mocked. 'And you meet a richer class of client in hotels like this one,' he added drily.

'The management would never allow it,' she dismissed, sure he had to be mocking her about the other woman's profession too. Miranda certainly hadn't looked like a prostitute. But then did they have to walk around in fish-net tights and snug-fitting clothes to be one? The answer was obviously no, especially in a hotel like this one. 'I had no idea . . .' she frowned.

Rogan shrugged. 'I travel around a lot, you soon get to recognise them.'

Caitlin's eyes suddenly widened indignantly. 'You surely didn't think that *I*——'

'Of course not.' His husky laugh taunted her. 'I told you I can recognise them, but that doesn't mean I'm ever interested in them. Bought sex isn't something I've ever had to resort to,' he added without conceit. 'When it is I'll consider myself too

old to be interested any more. No, I bought the lady
a drink and then politely left. She's only doing her
job, after all. As for you, I've already told you what I
think you are.'

'A bored married socialite looking for excitement
in my life,' she remembered disparagingly.

He tilted his head at her consideringly. 'Maybe
not a married one,' he conceded.

'But bored,' she snapped. 'A boredom you would
have been only too happy to help ease, I suppose?'

'More than happy,' he acknowledged, his eyes
brimming with laughter at her fury.

'How kind of you,' she said with saccharine
sweetness, rising gracefully to her feet, the blue
dress shimmering lovingly against her body to rest
just below her knees, high sandals the same shade of
blue elevating her height a good three inches. 'But
I'm afraid I'll have to decline your gracious offer,'
she looked pointedly towards the doors where a
man who was obviously her awaited mechanic
hesitated, the blue overalls stained with grease and
oil, although he was self-consciously trying to
straighten his hair as he became increasingly aware
of the elegance of his surroundings.

'I don't mind waiting,' Rogan drawled
suggestively.

She looked down at him coldly. 'I don't think you
will still be around in a hundred years!'

'Neither will you,' he reasoned.

'Exactly!' she said with satisfaction.

'Ouch!' He gave a pained wince.

'Goodbye, Mr McCord.' She nodded dismissively, a smile of welcome plastered on her face as she moved to greet the mechanic.

She took him outside to look at her car, listened for the next five minutes as he poked about under the bonnet talking about things she didn't even recognise the name of but which he talked about so lovingly she knew he understood what every single part of the engine should be doing—but obviously wasn't.

'What does it all mean?' She frowned when he at last straightened, wiping his hands on a cloth from his pocket.

The young man shrugged. 'It means I'm going to have to tow your car back to the garage and work on it there.'

That's what she had thought it meant! 'Thank you,' she sighed. 'I suppose I'd better go and organise a taxi——'

'No need for that,' cut in a voice that really was beginning to grate on her nerves.

Caitlin turned to Rogan McCord with icy eyes. 'What?' she bit out resignedly.

He strolled over to join them, enjoying a few minutes' consultation with the mechanic about her car before acknowledging her presence once again. 'I'll drive you home,' he stated arrogantly. 'I have my car over there.' He nodded in the direction of a dark grey Jaguar.

'Like hell——'

'Whew, English women aren't at all as cool and ladylike as they like to make out,' he confided in the mechanic. 'They aren't forgiving either.'

'What——'

'I offer to drive her home as an olive-branch after our argument and she throws it back in my face!' He shook his head, his expression pained.

It would be even more pained if he didn't stop giving the man who had introduced himself as Paul Raymond the impression the two of them were lovers who had just had a fight! They had certainly done nothing but fight since they first met, but they would never be lovers!

'I think you should accept the offer, Miss O'Rourke,' Paul Raymond advised softly.

'That's it, Paul,' Rogan grinned. 'We men have to stick together.'

The other man shot him an amused look. 'I'm sure you would be more comfortable in the Jag, Miss O'Rourke, than in the taxi.'

Rogan gave a mock groan of despair. 'Don't encourage her, she's already resorted to calling me names!'

The only name she had called him had been pirate, and that was proving even more true by the minute!

'Perhaps you're right, Paul.' She gave him a conspiratorial smile as she thought of the home she shared with her parents, and its distance from town. Rogan McCord was in for a surprise if he thought he just had to drive around London a bit to her home, where he would be invited up to her apartment for a nightcap as a thank-you for his kindness.

'Does that mean you accept my offer?' He

couldn't hide his surprise at her unquestioning compliance.

'Why not?' she agreed. 'Why look a gift-horse in the mouth, hmm, Paul.'

'Right, Miss O'Rourke,' the mechanic gave her a conspiratorial wink.

Rogan watched them frowningly. 'Why do I get the feeling I'm being outnumbered?'

'Probably because you are,' Caitlin mocked. 'Give me a call about the car, Paul,' she added warmly. 'Ready, Rogan?' she prompted tauntingly.

'Sure,' he nodded, unlocking the car door for her before climbing in beside her, lifting a hand in parting to the other man as he walked away to get his tow-truck. 'Where to now?' Rogan prompted as they reached the hotel exit.

'It will be simpler if I just direct you as we approach the correct roads,' she evaded, secretly wondering what on earth had prompted her to accept this lift home from a complete stranger. Bravado and vengeance, she finally decided. Bravado because Rogan McCord obviously thought he had the upper hand, vengeance because after the drive he would have to her home, with no return for his trouble once they got there, she doubted he would harass a woman the way he had her for some time to come. She decided the latter was well worth the uncertainty of trusting him at all!

After twenty minutes of driving, Caitlin could see he was starting to frown, five minutes later he began to scowl, five minutes after that he began to glower.

'Shouldn't be long now,' she told him cheerfully,

rubbing salt into the wound.

'Really?' he answered with barely concealed impatience, increasing the car's speed.

Caitlin grinned to herself, she had deliberately directed him to her home by the longest route possible, had even added a few detours to make it even longer. She was enjoying herself immensely.

'Do you work in London?' Rogan finally grated after another fifteen minutes' driving.

She nodded. 'I'm a nursery teacher.'

'It's a long trip to make each day.'

'Is it?' she widened innocently surprised eyes. 'I hadn't noticed.'

He shot her a look that was clearly sceptical, and Caitlin smiled back at him sweetly.

'Here we are,' she said a few minutes later, pointing to the entrance to the driveway that led to her home.

Rogan frowned, looking about him intently. 'I'm sure we've already been past here once tonight.'

She was glad of the darkness to hide her guilty blush. 'Don't be silly,' she dismissed briskly. 'Just park in front of the house,' she directed. 'It's a loop driveway so you can drive straight out again,' she added with satisfaction.

He parked the car in front of the huge oak doors, glancing up at the elegant Georgian-style house. 'Are you sure you aren't married?' he drawled. 'I'm sure you can't live here all alone.'

'I don't,' she confirmed. 'I live here with my parents. I'd love to invite you in,' she added with obvious insincerity, 'but it is late.' Because of all the detours they had taken! 'And I wouldn't like to disturb Mummy and Daddy.'

Rogan looked at the house again. 'I should think you could lose a person for a month in there and not hear their cries for help!'

'Mummy and Daddy are very light sleepers,' she taunted.

'Both of them?' he said drily.

'Yes.' She smiled her triumph. 'Thank you so much for driving me home, it was very kind of you.'

He turned in his seat, his arm coming to rest behind her shoulders. 'Kindness didn't come into it,' he drawled.

'I know,' she taunted, turning to open the door.

'Not so fast.' Rogan caught hold of her arm, pulling her towards him.

'What——?' Her question was never finished as his taunting mouth came down on hers.

Her head rested back on his arm as he leant over her, lost in the confines of his arms—and the magic of his lips. His shoulders felt smoothly powerful beneath her hands, his mouth moving against hers with insistent passion. He smelt of spicy soap and limes, his body warm as his shirt-covered chest pressed against her throbbing breasts.

His mouth became gently probing as he sensed her confused acquiescence, his lips moving moistly across her cheek as he told her how beautiful she was, how desirable, how much she excited him. Caitlin could feel herself being seduced by his verbal lovemaking, his green eyes piercing in the illumination from the lights beside the house doors, holding her captive as his mouth lowered to hers again.

They tasted, licked, nibbled, finally coming together with fierce passion, Rogan's hands restless on her body, at last lingering on the up-thrust of her breast.

Caitlin gasped as he sought, and found, the pointed tip, caressing softly, until the nipple firmed and throbbed for closer contact.

'I want to see you naked, Caity,' he told her gruffly as one of his hands moved to the zip on her gown. 'Naked and wanton!'

She felt hot, feverish—she was making love with a complete stranger!

'No!' She pulled out of his arms, her expression one of panic as he reached for her again. 'Let me go,' she instructed coldly.

Puzzlement darkened his eyes at her vehemence, but he sat back in his own seat, his hands held up defensively. 'I've never tried to force a woman,' he assured her raggedly.

She knew he had never needed to, that his brand of lovemaking could become addictive. 'I know that,' she conceded shakily, shaking back the fiery swathe of her hair. 'I—it was a mistake, that's all.'

Rogan shook his head, his eyes steely. 'I don't make mistakes, Caity. I want you. And a minute ago you wanted me too——'

'No,' she denied heatedly.' I told you, it was a mistake. I have to go in now.' She swallowed hard, wishing she had found the strength to go in earlier, much earlier.

He gave an abrupt inclination of his head. 'I'll be seeing you——'

'No,' she told him sharply, haltingly turning to look at him, realising how wrong she had been to let him know where her home was. He could cause so much trouble for her if he chose to! 'I don't want to see you again.'

'I'm afraid that's impossible.' He shook his head. 'You see, I——'

'You aren't listening to me! Can't you take no for an answer?' she snapped impatiently.

'You weren't saying no to me a few minutes ago,' he shrugged.

'Well, I'm saying it now,' Caitlin rasped. 'I don't want to see you ever again, Mr McCord. Do I make myself clear?'

'Very,' he drawled, very relaxed as he sat back in his seat watching her.

'Good.' Her eyes flashed before she stepped out on to the gravel driveway. 'Once again, thank you for the lift home.'

'Believe me, it was my pleasure,' he mocked. 'All of it.'

She slammed the door in his face, standing on the top step to watch the car—and Rogan McCord!— go out of the driveway before turning to enter the house.

As she had known they would be, her parents were still in the lounge, both of them night people, enjoying a game of chess together as she entered the room. They looked so endearingly familiar, her father so big and strong, her mother so small and feminine, that for a moment she was able to banish the madness she had known in Rogan McCord's arms as she returned their warm smiles.

When her mother smiled she didn't look much older than Caitlin, her hair as red as her daughter's despite her fifty years, her face beautiful and unlined. 'Did you have a nice evening, darling?'

'Not particularly.' She went on to tell them of the disappointing time she had had—omitting the part about Rogan McCord. That had been disturbing, not disappointing!

'What a shame,' her mother sympathised.

'Damned thoughtless, I call it,' her father bit out, he was a big bluff man of fifty-five, his hair having been iron-grey for as long as Caitlin could remember. Her brother Brian was hoping his brown hair would go the same colour so that he could look as distinguished as their father. 'Gayle could have called you,' he added with a frown.

Exactly what she had thought! 'I think I'll get off to bed now; I have a hectic day tomorrow.'

'Of course, dear.' Her mother smiled her sweetly serene smile.

The conversation with her parents had helped calm her a little, and she held off thoughts of Rogan McCord while she showered and changed for bed, although once she lay in the darkness he wouldn't be banished as easily; warm green eyes haunting her mind, that firmly sensuous mouth that could wreak such havoc with her senses, making her behave in a way she hadn't believed she was capable of.

She turned over with a sob, her breathing coming to a ragged halt as the moonlight gleamed on the white dress that hung outside her wardrobe. A wedding-dress. *Her* wedding-dress.

# CHAPTER TWO

IT had been a long and tiring day, her last at work for some time; she and Graham were going away for a two-week honeymoon after their wedding. But at least these two weeks with her new group of children for the year had helped cement a relationship that she hoped the children would remember until she returned. And by that time her name would have changed from O'Rourke to Simond-Smith. It was quite a mouthful for small children, but Graham's family wouldn't hear of using just Simond *or* Smith.

The last few weeks had been so hectic, but the weekend would see the culmination of all their plans. Saturday was her wedding day to Graham.

Caitlin had tried so hard not to think of Rogan McCord today, but it was difficult not to remember her wanton response to the man. She had wanted him to go on kissing and caressing her. Who knew where it might have ended if she hadn't come to her senses! She had blushed profusely at lunch-time when Paul Raymond had delivered her car to the school and asked if she had got home all right.

After that thoughts of Rogan had been impossible to put from her mind, and the last thing she felt like facing tonight was a family dinner party. But her mother had made the arrangements weeks ago, and she couldn't disappoint her. Besides, she needed this time with Graham, to sort out her feelings for him. God, it was a bit late in the day to start having doubts about their marriage now! But the disturbing memory of her response to Rogan McCord wouldn't go away.

'You look lovely, darling,' her mother complimented, entering Caitlin's bedroom after a brief knock.

She knew the black of her dress set off the fire of her hair, although that had been subdued to a burnished bronze by the loosely swept-up hair-style that left several loose tendrils framing the oval of her face. 'So do you.' She put her arm companionably through the crook of her mother's, several inches taller than the tiny woman at her side.

'Brian and Beth have arrived, but Graham rang a short time ago to say he would be slightly late; he's been delayed at the office,' she frowned. 'He and his parents should be here soon, though.'

Why did Graham have to be late tonight of all nights, when she needed to see him so badly!

'—your father was sure you wouldn't mind,' her mother was saying.

'I'm sorry, Mummy.' She shook her head with a guilty grimace. 'I wasn't listening.'

Her mother gave her an indulgent smile. 'Thinking about Saturday?'

'Yes,' she confirmed shakily.

Her mother squeezed her arm. 'You're going to be a beautiful bride.'

What woman wouldn't in the gown that had cost

a small fortune? Oh God, if only she had never met Rogan McCord!

'I was just explaining earlier that—well, you can see for yourself now,' her mother said brightly as they entered the lounge.

'See what for myself?' She frowned her puzzlement. 'Mummy, what——.'

'I think your mother was just trying to tell you that I'm their guest,' cut in an arrogantly mocking voice that she had hoped never to hear again!

All the colour drained from her cheeks as she turned to face her tormentor. Rogan was wearing a black dinner-suit and snowy white shirt tonight, but even those trappings of civilisation couldn't disguise his rakish, rather than polished, attraction.

What was he doing here? How had he managed to wangle an invitation to a family dinner from her father? By the look of the half empty glass in his hand he had been here for some time!

Before she could make any comment to his mocking statement Rogan put out his hand. 'I'm Rogan McCord,' he introduced himself unnecessarily. 'A business associate of your father's,' he added derisively.

He wasn't going to give her away to her family! *Why* wasn't he?

A business associate of her father's, he said. Since when? Today, perhaps? She looked at him suspiciously.

'Poor Rogan has been staying at a hotel the last few days,' her father put in sympathetically. 'I wouldn't hear of that continuing once he told me; I insisted he stay on here until our business is concluded.'

The two of them made that elegantly expensive hotel sound like the next thing up from a hovel! And she still didn't know how long this 'business association' had been going on.

Rogan was the one to answer that question. 'It was originally planned for me to see your father next week,' he explained. 'But I wound my business up in Germany much quicker than I expected to and came straight over.' His gaze levelled on her coldly. 'I had no idea I would be intruding on such an intimate family occasion.'

'You aren't intruding,' her father dismissed. 'We're glad to have you.'

'Miss O'Rourke?' Rogan prompted, his gaze fixed firmly on her flushed face.

'Any friend of my father's is most welcome,' she assured flatly.

'He's just invited me to attend the wedding, too,' he continued remorselessly. 'Saturday, isn't it?'

Oh God, now he must believe her to have been a panicked bride last night when she had responded to him so easily! 'Yes,' she rasped. 'Please do come, Mr McCord,' she regained some of her usual poise. 'We're hoping it will be a memorable occasion.'

'I'm sure it will be.' He gave an inclination of his head.

'Excuse me,' she said abruptly. 'I have to say hello to my brother and his wife.'

Saying hello to Brian and Beth took all of two minutes, by which time Rogan was ensconced on one of the sofas with her mother, the two of them deep in conversation. Surely he wouldn't—? No . . . Would he?

'What do you think of him, then, little sister?' Brian mused at her side, following her gaze as she watched Rogan charming their mother.

She sipped the dry sherry her father had brought over to her before answering, knowing how astute her brother could be at times. 'I don't really know much about him,' she shrugged uninterestedly.

Brian, tall and whipcord-thin, raised his brows over laughing blue eyes. 'You've never heard of Rogan McCord?'

Obviously not in the way her brother meant! 'Should I have done?' She sounded bored.

'He's a big shot in the real estate business,' Brian drawled. 'Although I think this is the first time he's ever ventured across the Atlantic.'

'And what lured him?' she asked.

'Dad, of course, and a partnership in a hotel chain they're both interested in,' Brian chuckled. 'The two of them met while Dad was in the States a few months ago. Of course your head has been too filled with wedding plans to be interested in the dry old family business, otherwise you would probably have heard all about him.'

Caitlin deliberately took the time to sip her sherry, not wanting her brother to see just how curious she was about the man who had been able to talk her father into a partnership in anything. 'Tell me now,' she invited softly, her eyes narrowing as Rogan made her mother giggle like a schoolgirl.

Her mother never *giggled*!

'Self-made man—they're always the toughest kind,' her brother said matter-of-factly. 'He's made a bundle over the years in property speculation.'

'That doesn't tell me anything about the man except that he's clever and shrewd,' she bit out. And she needed to know all there was to know about Rogan McCord, needed all the ammunition she could get.

'Sister dearest, you shouldn't *want* to know any more about the man; you're getting married on Saturday.'

'Brian!' his wife admonished as Caitlin blushed. Beth was a tiny blonde woman with warm brown eyes and a bubbly personality. 'Caity was merely interested. I must say I'm a little curious myself,' she added pointedly.

'Elizabeth O'Rourke, behave yourself!' her husband scowled.

Beth chuckled. 'I never realised what a jealous husband I was getting when I married a reformed rake!'

Caitlin shared in the humour at her brother's expense. Brian hadn't just been wild in his youth, he had been untameable, always smashing up his cars, their father always warning that this would be the last time—before he replaced the car yet again. Caitlin smiled as she remembered the parties Brian used to go to that lasted weeks rather than a single evening. And the women——! Even Brian had stopped counting them.

And then he had met Caitlin's school friend Beth.

He seemed to change overnight, sure that a sweetly beautiful girl like Beth wouldn't want a hell-raiser in her life. The month after they first met, Beth being eighteen to his twenty-seven, they had been married. Three years later they were happier than ever, and Caitlin's nephew, three-month-old Matthew, had completed that happiness.

Brian was a changed man, had joined their father in his considerable business interests as his assistant, and was now the successor their father had always wanted him to be. Caitlin didn't doubt that Brian was also a more contented man.

'You knew exactly what you were getting when you married me,' Brian said drily in answer to his wife's taunt. 'You realised the night I asked you to marry me and your old friend Jake asked you to dance and then held you too close for my liking.'

'Poor Jake saw stars for hours after you hit him!' Beth looked at her husband with indulgent affection.

'He was lucky to be able to see at all with that black eye,' Caitlin chuckled. 'I didn't appreciate having *my* date walking around looking like a panda all night because my brother acted like a caveman!'

'You told me you didn't like him that much, anyway,' Brian dismissed. 'You were just looking for a chance to get away from him.'

'I could hardly walk out on him after you'd hit him!' she pointed out drily.

'He should have kept his hands to himself,' Brian glowered at the memory.

'He did, *you* were the one that didn't,' Beth scolded. 'And stop changing the subject——'

'Me?' he said incredulously. 'You were the one——'

'He's just trying to avoid telling us about Rogan McCord,' Beth told Caitlin knowingly.

'What's to tell?' Brian dismissed impatiently. 'He's in his mid-thirties—and handsome as the devil!'

Beth smiled at her husband's disgruntled expression. 'So are you, darling.'

He sighed. 'You're just trying to humour me now.'

'Then stop acting like a baby,' ordered Beth. 'Is he married?'

'Rogan?' he frowned. 'I don't know why either of you should be interested in his marital status. You——'

'Brian!' Beth prompted firmly.

'No, he isn't married,' he told them irritably. 'Really, Beth, I don't know why——'

'Good evening.'

Caitlin turned sharply at the sound of that husky interruption, blue eyes clashing with green. She hadn't noticed Rogan leaving her mother's side as she and Beth engaged in one of their favourite pastimes, that of winding Brian up, but Rogan was standing all too close. She swallowed hard. 'Mr McCord,' she nodded, giving Beth and Brian an accusing look as they crossed the room to join her parents.

'I believe Rogan will do,' he drawled. 'And of course, you're Caitlin.'

She stiffened. 'Yes.'

'I told you we would meet again,' he told her challengingly.

Her eyes widened. 'You knew who I was all the time!'

'Not all the time, no,' he rasped. 'But as soon as I heard your name, yes. Your father told me about his beautiful daughter Caity when he was in the States earlier this year. He was quite right about your beauty.'

'Thank you,' she accepted tensely.

'He did forget to mention, however,' he continued slowly, 'that you're also wilful, spoilt—and a liar.'

'How dare you!' she gasped.

'How dare I?' He raised dark brows, his mouth thinning angrily. 'The drive that took us all of an hour last night took a mere twenty minutes this evening. Of course I knew that at the time, but I thought I'd let you have your little bit of fun——'

'You——'

'Don't add obscene language to your list of faults,' he bit out caustically. 'You were enjoying yourself,' he shrugged. 'And so I thought, what the hell? That takes care of wilful and spoilt,' he rasped. 'And tonight when I arrived your father told me he and your mother were just having a small family dinner party in honour of their daughter's wedding on Saturday. I thought he must have two daughters, but no, he told me there's only his Caity!' He looked at her disgustedly.

'So?' she challenged defiantly.

'So,' he was so close the warmth of his breath stirred the feathered fringe above her eyes, 'where was your engagement ring last night?'

'I'm not engaged,' she snapped. 'My family doesn't believe in them.' Mainly because they never knew their partners long enough to bother with them!

'You didn't act like a woman about to be married in five days!'

'*I* didn't act?' she repeated incredulously. 'You were the one who kissed me,' she hissed.

'And you kissed me right back!'

A guilty flush darkened her cheeks at the truth of that. 'You took me by surprise——'

'For fifteen minutes!' he derided harshly.

'Rogan, please,' she looked about them awkwardly, very conscious of where they were, and of her family in the room, even if he wasn't.

'Take me outside to look at the garden. Or something,' he instructed hardly, his eyes narrowed.

'No, I——'

'You would rather we continued with our conversation here?' he mocked tautly.

Brian and Beth were still talking with her parents on the other side of the lounge, but it was only a matter of time before they became curious about the intensity of the conversation between two supposed strangers. 'All right,' she agreed irritably. 'But

Graham and his parents will be arriving in a few minutes.' She hoped!

'The man you're going to marry?' Rogan prompted.

'Yes,' she confirmed defensively.

'I pity the poor bastard,' Rogan rasped as he accompanied her out on to the terrace that overlooked the gardens. 'God knows how you're going to behave *after* the two of you are married!'

'Will you keep your voice down?' She turned on him as soon as he had closed the door behind them, the September evening was warm, the sun not having gone down yet. 'Must I remind you that you were the one who kept following me last night,' she snapped agitatedly.

'All you had to do was calmly tell me you were getting married in five days' time; why didn't you?'

She had asked herself the same question all day, and not found a single answer. 'I don't know,' she admitted heavily.

'Caity——'

'Please don't.' She moved away from him as he would have enfolded her in his arms. 'I'm not proud of what happened last night, but I—I'll learn to live with it.'

'Why?' His eyes were narrowed to emerald slits, his hair taking on a blue-black sheen in the sunlight.

'Because I did respond to you,' she acknowledged gruffly. 'And I shouldn't have done.'

'Caity——'

'Let's go back inside.' Once again she avoided his arms. 'I heard a car just now; it must be Graham and his parents.' She deliberately evaded looking at him as he politely held the door open for her to enter.

The Simond-Smiths were just being shown into the lounge as the two of them entered from the garden, and Caitlin's eyes lit up as she saw Graham, reassured by his boyish smile, moving forward to receive his kiss before acknowledging his parents, Joanna and Peter, and his sister-in-law, Gayle.

Gayle kissed her on the cheek. 'I really am so sorry about last night. I was helping Graham with some research for his book, and it completely slipped my mind that I'd arranged to meet you.'

The other woman had telephoned her first thing this morning to apologise for the oversight, and once she had heard the reason she had forgiven Gayle for the lapse; the book Graham was writing on the Vikings was absorbing stuff. An accountant by profession, in partnership with his father, Graham had a passion for Viking history.

'Please don't worry about it,' she tucked her hand into the crook of Graham's arm, 'I know how carried away Graham can get over his book.' She gave him an indulgent smile.

'Aren't you going to introduce us, Caity?'

She glared at Rogan as he used the term of affection deliberately. 'Graham Simond-Smith, and his sister-in-law, Gayle,' she bit out tautly. Graham's parents were in conversation with her own and Brian and Beth, leaving them a curious quartet. 'A business acquaintance of my father's, Rogan McCord,' she supplied pointedly.

His handshake with Graham was brief to say the least, Caitlin's mouth tightening as Graham gave a perplexed frown at the other man's coldness, looking completely baffled by his own treatment as Rogan gave Gayle a smile of lingering charm.

Caitlin wasn't puzzled at all by his behaviour; she knew that he despised Graham as much as he pitied him, believing she treated the other man as a fool. And he couldn't help turning his charm on Gayle, who, widowed for the last two years, was still very young and beautiful.

Gayle had been married to Graham's older brother, and continued to live in the family home even after his death at the end of a long illness. Caitlin had never known Thomas Simond-Smith, but she knew Graham had admired his brother tremendously, and that Gayle hadn't looked at another man since his death.

Until now! Gayle couldn't help but look at Rogan McCord as he drew her away to talk quietly together in one of the bay windows fronting the house. Gayle was blushing prettily at what Rogan was saying to her, reminding Caitlin that the other woman was still only thirty years old, even though her widowhood occasionally made her seem much older.

'Who is he?' Graham frowned as he watched the other man across the room.

'I told you, a business associate of my father's,' she dismissed, turning her back on the other couple. 'How about a proper hello; I haven't seen you for two days!' she teased.

He grinned down at her, looking younger than his twenty-six years, his blond hair, kept cut short because of its tendency to curl, in need of the cut it was undoubtedly going to get on the morning before their wedding, falling untidily on to his forehead.

He was young and uncomplicated, and Caitlin had been attracted to him from the moment they met a year ago. Happily he had returned the attraction, and they had both looked forward to their wedding-day.

Had. Caitlin stole a glance at Rogan and Gayle as she and Graham strolled out into the garden; the other woman was totally engrossed in Rogan's drawled words. Caitlin wondered what they were talking *about*.

'Mmm.' Graham drew his head back to gaze down at her with warm eyes, his hands linked at the base of her spine as he held her to him after their lingering kiss. 'I've missed you.'

'I've missed you too.' This time she kissed him with a fierceness that bordered on desperation.

'Hey!' Graham straightened, a flush to his cheeks. 'Someone could come out to call us for dinner at any moment.'

'Someone already has,' rasped a harsh voice, Rogan's gaze cold as it flickered over Caitlin's dishevelled hair and slightly swollen lips. 'Your mother said dinner is about to be served. Unless you would like me to tell them you've decided not to bother?' he added suggestively.

A dark flush heated her cheeks. 'Please tell Mummy we'll be right there,' she snapped.

'Who *is* he?' Graham muttered once again when they were alone.

'Just someone Daddy felt obliged to invite to stay.' She walked apart from him back to the house.

'He makes me feel about ten years old,' Graham told her uncomfortably.

'Don't be silly,' Caitlin dismissed brittly, knowing the feeling only too well!

'He almost makes me feel guilty for slipping out to the garden to kiss the woman who is almost my wife,' he said in a disgruntled voice as they re-entered the lounge.

'Just forget about him,' she advised, knowing that was going to be impossible with Rogan in this baiting mood.

Not that there was much evidence of that as he concentrated his attention on Gayle throughout dinner. Caitlin was very quiet, as was Graham, still resentful of the other man's condescension if his glowering looks in Rogan's direction were anything to go by.

But Gayle flowered under the undivided attention of such an attractive man, her blue eyes sparkling her enjoyment, even her dark cap of hair seeming to take on a new vibrancy. No one else but Caitlin and Graham seemed aware of the friction at the oval table, Brian and Beth enjoying themselves as usual, the two sets of parents talking over the last-minute details of the wedding.

For a bride and groom they were singularly lacking in enthusiasm for this discussion!

'I wonder what Graham would say if he knew

that last night *I* was the one kissing you and receiving that passionate response that frightened the hell out of him!'

Rogan had moved to stand behind her as Graham went to get her an after-dinner brandy, having been delayed returning to her as her brother waylaid him, teasing him about the wedding Saturday if the good-natured laughter was anything to go by.

She turned sharply to Rogan. 'It didn't frighten him,' she defended. 'He was naturally cautious about our location!'

'Like you were last night when we sat outside your parents' home?'

'Please keep your voice down!' She looked about them uncomfortably, returning her father's smile shakily as she caught his gaze on them.

Rogan shrugged. 'I should think it would mess up all those expensive wedding plans somewhat if I were to mention who you were with last night.'

'You wouldn't.' She frowned her distress. 'Tell me you wouldn't, Rogan!'

'I wouldn't,' he repeated obediently.

'You would!' she groaned, closing her eyes, a deeper blue when she opened them again. 'Do you have any idea how long my mother has been planning this wedding?' she accused.

'Since you were in your cradle, probably,' he drawled uninterestedly.

'Longer,' she said flatly. 'Brian was supposed to have been a girl. It was another nine years before I came along.'

'And you've been spoilt ever since,' Rogan
grated. 'Did no one ever explain to you that you
can't have your cake and eat it as well?'

Her eyes widened indignantly. 'You must have
heard Gayle say *she* was the person I was supposed
to be meeting last night!'

'I also heard you telling Graham how you missed
him last night,' Rogan taunted. 'You didn't seem to
be coping too badly when we were together.'

She shot another frantic look about the room.
'We were not *together*,' she snapped.

'Don't kid yourself—or me, Caity,' he rasped.
'Another couple of minutes and we would have
been making love on the front seat of my car in front
of your parents' house!'

'No!' She shook her head in firm denial.

Rogan gave her a scathing glance. 'I know damn
well that you wanted me.'

'No. I——'

'Here we are, Caitlin.' Graham finally arrived
back with their drinks, looking at the other man
with questioning eyes as he noticed Caitlin's
flushed face. 'Sorry, old man, I only brought two
glasses,' he dismissed smugly.

'That's all right—son,' grated Rogan, taking both
glasses of brandy out of the other man's hand,
giving one to Caitlin and keeping the other one for
himself. 'I'm sure Caity and I can amuse ourselves
while you get yourself a drink.'

Good manners warred with indignation in
Graham's good-looking face, the former winning
out as he left them with a mumbled 'excuse me'.

Rogan raised dark brows at Caitlin as she demurely sipped her brandy. 'No comment?'

She shrugged. 'Graham doesn't like you.'

The feeling is mutual,' he bit out, his eyes narrowed as he watched the other man. 'I wonder why that is?'

She turned away. 'I have no idea.'

'Don't you?' Rogan taunted.

Her face became flushed. 'The time to make trouble for me was when we were first introduced, not now!' She glared at him.

'Oh, I don't intend making trouble for you, Caity,' he drawled.

'No?' she scorned.

'No,' he confirmed calmly. 'I'm sure that in the end you'll make the only decision that you can in the circumstances.'

She frowned. 'There's no decision to make; I'm going to marry Graham on Saturday.'

Dark brows rose over mocking eyes. 'Why bother, when you'll be unfaithful to him within a couple of months?'

Her eyes flashed. 'You don't know what you're talking about——'

'Don't I?' he challenged softly, one lean hand moving up to caress her cheek. 'I can assure you I do, you see *I'll* be the man you're unfaithful with! It's going to be worth hanging around in England just for that,' he taunted.

'You arrogant——'

'Darling, Gayle isn't feeling too well.' A worried-looking Graham rejoined them. 'Her head's pounding, so I've offered to take her home,' he explained further.

'I'm so sorry,' a pale-faced Gayle stood at his side, 'I don't mean to break up the party.'

'You aren't,' Caitlin reassured her sympathetically. 'What you need is some aspirin and a good night's sleep.'

'But I don't like to drag Graham away, tonight of all nights.' Gayle still looked worried.

'I shouldn't worry about that, Gayle,' Rogan drawled. 'After Saturday Caitlin is going to have all of Graham's nights for the rest of their lives.' He looked challengingly at Caitlin before turning back to the other woman. 'Perhaps it isn't fair to part the happy couple, after all,' he mocked. 'I'll drive you home, if you like, Gayle.'

'Oh, but——'

'Something wrong, old man?' Rogan quirked dark brows at Graham's protest.

'Yes! No! Well—er——' He looked at Gayle, his face flushed. 'Is that all right with you?' he asked her lamely.

Gayle smiled shyly at Rogan. 'If you're sure you don't mind?'

'What sane man would mind taking home a beautiful woman?' he flirted huskily.

Caitlin could have groaned at the sugary flattery, although Gayle didn't seem to mind it; she was ready to leave with him within a few minutes, and the family gathered around the doorway to watch them depart.

Caitlin's father suddenly began to chuckle. 'Now

I realise how Rogan got his nickname,' he explained at the questioning looks he received. 'He certainly is a fast worker!'

Caitlin stiffened warily. 'Oh?'

'Oh yes,' her father grinned. 'In the States they call him The Rogue because he's such a devil with the ladies. I should keep a sharp eye on him with Gayle, if I were you, Peter, he . . .'

Caitlin didn't hear any more, too lost in her own humiliating thoughts. A 'rogue', and 'a devil with the ladies', was he! And a man like that had tried to persuade her to call off her wedding to Graham. Rogue was too kind a description for what Rogan McCord was!

# CHAPTER THREE

'I KNEW you would look like this.'

Caitlin spun around as Rogan softly closed the bedroom door behind him, indignation battling with the heat that suffused her body at the way he looked at her so intimately, lingering over every detail of her appearance. Her hair had been brushed and secured in a ponytail at the crown of her head, her face cleansed of make-up, the dark blue nightgown she wore making her eyes apear the same colour. She realised how sheer the nightgown was as Rogan's gaze lingered on each creamy curve. To her chagrin she felt her nipples harden and thrust forward, dark circles against the material.

'You know, without all that sophisticated make-up, and those designer-label gowns, you look more beautiful than ever,' he told her gruffly.

She drew in a controlling breath; she had been about to climb into bed when he walked in unnannounced, the bedclothes turned back invitingly. 'I'm afraid you have the wrong room, Mr McCord,' she bit out frostily. 'I'm afraid I don't know which bedroom my parents have put you in, but I can ring for——'

'Don't ring for anyone, Caity,' he warned softly. 'I have the right bedroom.'

Her cheeks coloured brightly. 'I don't think so,

Mr McCord. Now, if you wouldn't mind . . .'

'I have no intention of leaving here until you assure me you aren't going to marry Graham Simond-Smith!' he bit out grimly.

She gasped back the angry retort that sprang to her lips at his arrogance, instead speaking softly, so as not to disturb her parents or Beth and Brian in their bedrooms further up the corridor, if just as angrily. 'My wedding arrangements have nothing whatsoever to do with you, Mr McCord,' she snapped.

'As the man you really want I think they have everything to do with me!'

'The man I——!' She gave a disbelieving laugh. 'The sort of lust you evoke is far removed from my feelings for Graham!'

'Lust?' he repeated, dangerously soft. 'I made love to you last night!'

'Would The Rogue know the difference?' she taunted.

Rogan sighed, moving further into the room, pulling loose his bow-tie with impatient movements. 'Your father has been gossiping,' he grimaced.

Caitlin shook her head, eyeing him warily as his jacket followed his bow-tie on to her bedroom chair. 'Just warning Graham's father to watch out for you with the ladies. How is Gayle, by the way?' she asked pointedly, knowing it had been over two hours since he had left with the other woman.

'She has a migraine,' he replied censoriously. 'I sat with her until the family arrived home.'

'How thoughtful of you,' Caitlin taunted, concerned for Gayle, but doubting Rogan's motives had been as innocent as he made out they were.

He shrugged. 'I thought so, but it's obvious you—— My God, is this your wedding-dress.' His attention had been caught by the yards and yards of glowing white satin.

'No,' she answered drily. 'It's my bathrobe!'

Rogan shot her a scathing glance for her sarcasm, striding across the room to touch the dress almost reverently. 'You would have looked lovely in it,' he murmured throatily.

'Thank you—— What do you mean, *would have*?' she realised sharply.

'So many brides don't have the right to wear white nowadays; do you?' He ignored her question.

'That's none of your business!' She slapped his hand away from her dress. 'What do you mean, would have?' she repeated heatedly.

'Well, you'll never have a chance to wear it now,' he dismissed arrogantly.

'Who says I won't?' Caitlin demanded furiously.

Rogan's mouth twisted mockingly. 'I do.'

Her cheeks were flushed. 'It might interest you to know I don't care what you say!'

Rogan shrugged dismissively. 'I'm sure you're very fond of Graham——'

'How kind of you to say so—when Saturday is our wedding-day!' Her eyes glittered deeply blue.

'But it isn't.' Rogan calmly shook his head. 'Being fond of someone isn't enough to base a marriage on.'

'I think you're underestimating my feelings for Graham,' she snapped.

'Women in love do not respond to another man,' he told her firmly.

'Not even if the "other man" is that accomplished rake, The Rogue?' she taunted, stung by his arrogance.

His face darkened with irritation. 'I earned that name when I was at school and bedding every female who would let me,' he scowled. 'Unfortunately the media picked it up once I was visible in business.'

'You mean it isn't true?' Caitlin sympathised acidly. 'You're just a poor misunderstood man looking for love in his life!'

He gave a self-derisive grin. 'Not quite,' he conceded drily.

'I thought not,' she bit out. 'Now will you please take yourself *and* your notorious reputation out of my bedroom?'

He shook his head. 'Not until I've talked some sense into you.'

She blinked at his arrogance. 'I could always scream,' she threatened. 'I estimate an average of eight people would come running to my room to see what was wrong,' she challenged.

'Would you really want that?' Rogan reasoned, sitting on the side of the bed.

'Would you?' she returned sharply. 'I believe you and my father are in the middle of negotiating a partnership,' she added pointedly.

His face darkened. 'Nothing has been decided yet.'

'Well, I can assure you that coming to my room like this isn't going to endear you to him at all!'

He held up his hands defensively. 'I only came to talk, you're the one walking around half-naked.' His gaze moved slowly over her body covered only by the sheer material of her nightgown.

'Would you get out of here!' She picked up his jacket and bow-tie and threw them at him, further enraged when he let them fall to the floor, furiously picking them up from where he had let them fall beside the bed to throw them at him again. 'You—what are you doing?' she gasped as her wrist was grasped by lean fingers and she was pulled down on top of his chest, the heat of his flesh through the silk shirt searing her body. 'Rogan, let me go,' she ordered breathlessly, mesmerised by slumberous green eyes.

'I can't!' he groaned, rolling over to take her with him so that she lay sprawled on the bed beneath him. 'I tried talking to you, but you wouldn't listen, and now I couldn't talk if you gave me a million dollars!'

He had warned her, but even so she wasn't prepared for the warm sensuality of his mouth as it moved over hers, feeling an instant response, her arms moving up of their own volition to encircle his neck.

His skin felt firm and slightly damp to the touch, muscles rippling beneath the surface of that smooth flesh as one of his hands moved between her and the bed, arching her body into his.

His mouth felt like satin, his tongue a heady rasp
as it probed the hollows of her throat; her breasts
bared to that questing mouth and searching tongue
as Rogan eased the ribbon straps of her gown down
her arms to pull the silky material to her waist.

For long agonising moments she lay with her eyes
closed, clinging to him mindlessly as the erotic
sensation of a suckling mouth at her nipples washed
over her. Heat engulfed her body, her lids flying
open in alarm, and then wonder, as that hand closed
over her womanhood, the silk of her gown a caress
against the aching nub of her desire.

The heat became almost unbearable as she
watched his mouth move against her breasts, dark
lashes fanning cheeks flushed with desire. Her
hands moved to cradle the back of his head, holding
him against her, crying out at the deep ache of
pleasure that engulfed her as she felt the gentle nip
of his teeth, quickly followed by the soothing rasp of
his tongue.

She reacted instinctively, her caresses fevered,
needing to touch him as he was touching her, loving
the throbbing hardness of him as she touched his
thighs, encouraged by the low groan in his throat as
one of her hands slipped beneath the material that
covered him.

His response couldn't be doubted as he moved
against her, like satin to the touch, although the
power beneath that silky softness promised much
pleasure.

'No more,' Rogan finally gasped, moving away

from her to throw off the rest of his clothes, slowly working her crumpled nightdress down her thighs and on to the floor, lying across her now as he moved up to claim her mouth once more.

As she felt the velvet shaft of him probing against her softness the reality of what she had allowed to happen washed over her, and as she felt him start to enter her she began to panic. 'Stop!' She pushed at his chest. 'Rogan, no!' she pleaded as he would have surged completely into her.

He hesitated, his eyes burning with his need as he looked into her pale face. 'No?' he managed to probe harshly.

She swallowed hard, breathing raggedly, knowing how close they were to being completely one. 'Please don't,' she choked.

He was breathing hard, his elbows supporting him as he lay on top of her, her body still open to him. 'You want me!'

'Yes, but Saturday is supposed to be my wedding day! And——'

'And you *still* mean to go through with that?' Rogan straightened forcefully, looking down at her disgustedly. 'Don't you realise that what happens between us when we touch is special?'

Stark reality had left Caitlin pale and trembling, and she stood up to wrap a towelling robe about her to hide her naked vulnerability from Rogan. 'Special in the way that you've never shared a woman's bed under her parents' roof before?' she scorned, her arms wrapped about herself as she trembled with emotion. 'Believe me, I've never been to bed with a man under my parents' roof before either!'

A nerve pulsed in his jaw, his eyes as cold as ice. 'I didn't mean that to happen, damn you,' he rasped. 'I came here to talk to you, but the only way I seem to be able to communicate with you is to make love to you!'

'Rogan, you——'

His eyes glittered. 'Maybe that *is* the only way a man can communicate with you!'

An angry flush darkened her cheeks. 'The extent of my sexual experience is none of your business——'

'Sweetheart, I *know* the extent of your sexual experience,' he scorned. 'You know every little trick there is to drive a man insane!'

Caitlin gasped at the unfairness of that remark. She had caressed him instinctively, not in a practised way, had no idea how much she had pleased him until his admission just now. 'And I suppose your morals are to be highly recommended?' she taunted angrily. 'A man offers you the hospitality of his home and you decide to take his daughter too!'

A dark flush coloured his cheeks. 'I told you, I didn't mean that to happen!'

'Must I remind you that this is *my* bedroom, that *you* came in here uninvited, that you *insisted* on staying even when I asked you to leave?' she snapped, her eyes blazing. 'As I'm *ordering* you to do now,' she added fiercely.

He stood up to pull on his clothes. 'Don't worry,

I'm going!' he rasped. 'If you want to enter into a marriage that can't possibly succeed that's your problem.'

'Exactly!' she glared at him fiercely. 'I—— What do you think you're doing?' she demanded as he opened the door and went out into the corridor.

'What does it look like?' he bit out. 'You wanted me to leave, so I'm leaving.'

'You could have checked the hallway first,' she hissed. Anyone in the family could have come along and seen him leaving her bedroom, her parents not having long gone to bed themselves, and Brian, Beth and Matthew were staying the night too.

Caitlin reached the doorway of her room just in time to look out and see a stony-faced Rogan entering a room further up the corridor, without even a backward glance in her direction.

'Couldn't you sleep, darling?' Her mother's gentle query made her give a guilty start of surprise. 'I'm sorry, Caity,' she smiled at her panicked reaction, 'I didn't mean to startle you.'

'It's all right, Mummy.' She gave a wan smile, her heart beating loudly. 'And no, I couldn't sleep.'

'We have a busy day ahead of us tomorrow,' her mother nodded. 'I couldn't sleep myself. I was just going downstairs to make a cup of cocoa. Would you like to join me?'

Caitlin sighed as she accompanied her mother into the kitchen. 'It's all been such a lot of hard work for you, hasn't it?'

'I didn't mind,' her mother assured her with a smile. 'In a way it's been my dream wedding as much as yours. Your father and I eloped, you know,' she recalled with a dreamy sigh.

Caitlin did know. It was probably the first, and last, impulsive thing her father had ever done! Her father had carried her mother off in the face of her family's objections, but the proof of their love for each other had been thirty-two years of happy marriage. All of her family had happy marriages, and while she didn't doubt that being married to Graham would be a comfortable feeling, she had come to realise during the last few days that comfort was what you wanted from clothes or a bed, not from a husband.

It was very late by the time she and her mother parted outside her room, and their talk had done nothing to ease her tortured thoughts and self-recriminations.

She had been mere seconds away from being totally possessed by Rogan, could even now feel the way he had gently probed against her. God, she didn't think that memory would ever leave her!

# CHAPTER FOUR

CAITLIN gave Storm free rein as he galloped across the meadows forming part of her parents' estate, so light on his hoofs he seemed not to notice he carried her weight on his back. He was a magnificent animal, a gift from Brian and Beth on her twenty-first birthday earlier in the year. Her parents had been horrified by the size of the magnificent beast as he pawed the ground outside their home, but Caitlin had run laughingly into Brian and Beth's arms to thank them for their wonderful gift.

She and Storm had been inseparable since the day Brian and Beth gave him to her, and although Graham didn't share her love of horses so enthusiastically he had agreed when she suggested they look for a home with stables.

Graham. Only three days left before their wedding.

It was only just after dawn now, but she had been unable to lie in bed any longer, and she could see Storm from her bedroom window as he snorted impatiently in the pasture next to the house. With Storm beneath her and the breeze in her hair she could quite well believe she didn't have a care in the world.

Until the person causing all the unrest in her life loomed darkly on the horizon!

Rogan rode her father's chestnut mare, not dressed in the traditional riding-gear as she was, but instead looking a little like a ranch-hand, without the hat, his denims faded and snug-fitting, a leather jacket worn over a checked shirt, muddy boots resting in the stirrups. His hair had been blown about by the crisp early morning breeze, falling darkly over his forehead as he rode up to join her on top of the hill overlooking the house. After last night Caitlin was even more wary of him.

'I watched you leave from my bedroom window.' He reined in next to her, his eyes narrowed. 'When you didn't seem in a hurry to come back I thought I would ride out and join you.'

'Why?' she said bluntly. Didn't he know—or care!—that he had completely disrupted her life!

Rogan sighed. 'I said some pretty harsh things to you last night——'

'Really?' she cut in tautly. 'I consider everything you've ever said to me an insult!'

'Damn you, Caity,' he grabbed hold of her reins as she would have ridden off, 'I've just spent a sleepless night imagining you walking down the aisle to Graham Simond-Smith on Saturday, and you aren't leaving here until I've had my say.'

'*You've* spent a sleepless night?' she scorned. 'My life was all planned out until you came along!'

His eyes were narrowed to emerald slits. 'And that's what you want, an ordered life?'

'And what's wrong with that?' *Everything*, the rebellious ache inside her told her. 'It's better than being just another notch in the bedpost of an accomplished and despicable rake!'

He ran a hand through the dark thickness of his hair, controlling the impatient gelding with ease. 'I told you I earned that reputation at school,' he rasped. 'I'm thirty-six now, not a kid out to prove himself.'

'Rogan, how many men do you know who can recognise a prostitute on sight?' she sighed.

'That's what you have against me, the fact that I know a hooker when I see one?'

'Of course not,' she denied impatiently. 'But can't you see your timing is all wrong?'

'On the contrary, I think my timing was just right,' he scorned. 'If I had arrived next week as I originally planned I would have been too late to stop you making the biggest mistake of your life!'

'My marriage to Graham,' she guessed drily.

'Of course your marriage to Graham,' he bit out impatiently. 'He's probably a very good man, would make a faithful husband. But he isn't for you. I'm telling you one last time, call off your wedding to him.'

Her eyes widened at his arrogance. 'You're *telling* me?' she repeated softly.

'Don't act the high-born lady with me, Caity,' he ground out. 'You don't love Graham, and we both know it.'

She did love Graham, although she knew she didn't *desire* him with the burning ache that was never far below the surface when she was with this man. 'We don't *both* know anything of the sort,' she dismissed coolly. 'Now if you wouldn't mind,' she released her reins from his grasp, 'I'm meeting Graham in a few minutes.'

Rogan's eyes narrowed. 'Can't stay away from each other, hmm?'

Her mouth twisted. 'We happen to care about each other!'

He looked angered by the claim. 'Are you going to tell him the wedding is off or not?'

'I'm not.' She shook her head.

'You're making a mistake, Caity,' he told her softly. 'A big mistake.'

Her eyes widened. 'Are you threatening me?'

He threw back his head and laughed. 'If I were you, I would probably spit in my face.'

'I stopped doing that when I started school. The teachers convinced me it wasn't at all ladylike,' she mocked.

'Is that where they also taught you that a socially acceptable marriage is everything?'

Her mouth firmed at his derision. 'It's where they warned us about rakes like you!'

He sighed raggedly. 'I'm not a rake, damn it!' he ground out.

'No?' she taunted scornfully. 'When did you last go to bed with a woman?'

A dark flush coloured his cheeks as he drew in a harsh breath. 'Caity, you——'

'When, Rogan?' she mocked.

He gave an impatient sigh. 'In Germany,' he finally muttered.

'I said when, not where,' she dismissed softly.

'It—I—— Four days ago,' he admitted forcefully

in the face of her insistence.

'And the time before that?' She quirked auburn brows over innocently candid eyes.

'That has nothing to do——'

'Just answer the question, Rogan,' she sighed a little impatiently.

'About a week before that, in the States,' he told her irritably. 'But——'

'There's no need to make excuses, Rogan,' she derided.

'I'm not making excuses!' he rasped.

'And why should you, any healthy male would feel proud to have bedded two different women in as many weeks. Now let's see, there are fifty-two weeks in a year, and I would say you've been sexually active . . .' she looked at him consideringly, 'probably twenty-two years of your life——'

'Twenty-one,' he ground out.

She nodded. 'Fifty-two times twenty-one is——'

'Wrong,' he scowled. 'Completely wrong. The woman in Los Angeles is a friend. We just——'

'Occasionally sleep together,' Caitlin said understandingly. 'How often do you see her?'

He shrugged. 'Every couple of weeks or so. But——'

'Okay, we'll give you the benefit of the doubt and say twenty-six times twenty-one,' Caitlin told him lightly. 'That's a total of five hundred and forty-six.' Her eyes widened. 'That isn't bad for an unmarried man. Some married men I know would tell you *they* would be grateful for a count like that, I'm sure!'

'How well do you *know* them?' Rogan rasped.

'Really, Rogan.' She shook her head. 'Don't try and label everyone else with your sexual appetite.'

A ruddy hue darkend his cheeks. 'I sometimes go for months without sex,' he defended. 'I certainly haven't been to bed with five hundred and forty-six different women!'

'Even a quarter of that number would have to place you in the rake category,' Caitlin scorned. 'And I am not about to throw away my marriage to Graham because you want to add me to their number!'

'Caity, I wouldn't ask it if I didn't think we have something special between us!'

She looked at him disbelievingly. 'Are you saying you're in love with me, that *you* want to marry me?'

'Hell, no,' he looked taken aback by the suggestion, 'I've tried marriage.'

Caitlin looked at him with new eyes. 'You have?'

'Yes. I didn't like it.'

From his expression the experience had been far from a happy one! 'Maybe your wife objected to "The Rogue" reputation,' she said drily.

'That had nothing to do with it, she—— Caity, I don't want to talk about my marriage——'

'Why not?' she raised her brows. 'You've done nothing else *but* talk about mine!'

'That's different.'

'Why? Because you say it is?' she derided. 'Rogan, I'm flattered by the interest you've taken in my happiness—especially as you were offering me an affair yourself not two days ago,' she mocked. 'But it really is unnecessary for you to trouble yourself. I think I am the best judge of what will make me happy.'

'And it isn't me,' he rasped.

She laughed huskily, holding Storm steady after turning him. 'It most certainly isn't!' She nudged Storm into a gallop, bending low over his neck as they jumped a couple of fences on their way back to the stables.

When she slipped down off the gelding's back in the courtyard and turned to look up at the hillside it was to find Rogan still sitting there watching her. She felt a shiver down her spine at his stillness, like a premonition, feeling even more uneasy as he urged the mare towards the house.

The shower washed the smell of the stables from her hair and body, the reflection of her wedding-dress seeming to mock her as she dried her hair in front of the mirror.

Damn Rogan McCord for unsettling her in this way. It had been all settled — the wedding, where they were to live, even the children they would eventually like to have.

While she had been out for her ride the maid had been in to tidy her room, and several newly pressed things left in the wardrobe ready to take on her honeymoon. She paused to touch the filmy white nightgown that hung amongst the clothes, the gown she would wear for her wedding-night.

She had dreamt of her wedding-day ever since she was a child, when her mother had woven the fantasy of her walking down the aisle to her Prince Charming. She had been out with plenty of other men before Graham, but it hadn't taken her long to decide he was the man she wanted to be waiting for her at the end of that aisle. She hadn't expected a rogue like Rogan McCord to come along and try to ruin that image for her!

Her hand moved sharply away from the night-gown, time passing quickly while she indulged in her daydreams, and she was supposed to be meeting Graham at eight o'clock before he had to go in to work and they both became caught up in the rush of the day.

It was a short drive to their agreed meeting place, but Caitlin had barely left the driveway to her parents' house when she noticed the dark grey Jaguar behind her in her driving-mirror. Rogan was following her!

The arrogant——!

She put her foot down on the accelerator, giving a satisfied smile as he had to do the same, the Jaguar staying just behind her. She didn't know what he hoped to achieve by following her, but if he wanted a chase he was going to get one!

It was still quite early for traffic to be too heavy on this midweek morning, and what little there was the two of them weaved in and out of with increasing daring. Caitlin smiled gleefully at Rogan's grim expression when she glanced in the driving-mirror at him, the smile turning to a frown as Rogan manoeuvred the Jaguar up beside her and forced her to take a turn-off on to a minor road. She swerved precariously round the corner, knew Rogan, beside her, would have hit any traffic coming the other way. If there had been any. Which there wasn't. But Rogan couldn't have been sure of that, damn him!

Suddenly it was no longer funny, this mad chase, and she turned off into a parking area amongst some trees, getting out of the car to stride over to where Rogan still sat in the idling Jaguar.

'You could have been killed back there!' she stormed, a cream blouse tucked into the waistband of cream trousers, a large cameo brooch pinned at the high collar of the blouse, her hair loose down her back.

'I don't think so,' he taunted. 'From my vantage point I could see around the corner.'

'Your vantage point was the wrong side of the road!' she glared.

'Would you have cared?' he mocked, getting out of the car to lean back against the door.

Her eyes flashed. 'I may not like you very much, Mr McCord, but even I wouldn't want—— What are you doing?' She frowned as he moved to the boot of his car and took out two suitcases. 'You can't—— Those are *my* suitcases!' she realised with a gasp as he took out the second two and placed them next to what were obviously his own suitcases.

Rogan nodded. 'All neatly packed and ready to go. Even down to the new toothbrushes.' He easily carried two of the cases across to her car and put them in the boot, going back for the second two while Caitlin dazedly looked in at her own rapidly filling boot.

'But why?' she gasped her confusion.

Rogan looked at her with narrowed green eyes. 'Why do I have my suitcases with me?' He shrugged. 'Because I'm leaving, of course. None of the family was up when I left, so I entrusted a note to the butler telling your father I've been called away on business.'

'I don't give a damn about that,' she snapped impatiently. 'The sooner you leave the better as far as I'm concerned! I want to know what you're doing with *my* suitcases?' she demanded infuriatedly.

'I didn't think you would appreciate not having along a change of clothes.' He held her car door open for her, Caitlin complying automatically, watching as he walked around to get in beside her.

'Those cases probably contain half my trousseau!' she told him scathingly.

'Probably,' he nodded. 'It all looked very nice. Now, are you going to drive or am I?' He quirked dark brows.

'Drive?' she repeated tautly. 'Drive where?'

His mouth twisted, he relaxed back in the seat as he raised one knee to rest it against the dashboard. 'It will be simpler if I just direct you as we approach the right roads,' he drawled mockingly.

An angry flush darkened her cheeks as he reminded her of the way she had tricked him that first evening when he drove her home. 'I'm not driving anywhere until you tell me *where* we're going,' she bit out stubbornly.

Rogan sighed. 'Where's your sense of adventure? Your feel for romance?'

'Waiting for an answer — as I am,' she retorted drily.

'Okay,' he grimaced. 'If you want to spoil the surprise ... I'm taking you away from all this.'

'"All this" being?' she derided.

Rogan shrugged. 'It's quite simple, Caity, I've kidnapped you. If after a couple of days with me you still want to return to Graham and go through with the wedding then you'll be able to, but for the next few days you're mine.' He gave a self-satisfied smile. 'You wanted a pirate—well, now you've got one!'

## CHAPTER FIVE

'YOU'LL never get away with it,' Caitlin gave a self-confident shake of her head.

'Strange, I thought I already had,' he taunted.

Perhaps it was a ridiculous statement to have made in the circumstances; she had refused to drive the two of them anywhere, and so he had taken charge behind the wheel himself, the two of them even now speeding towards London. But managing to drive her into London and succeeding in keeping her with him once they arrived were two totally different things!

'Don't look so worried, Caity,' he drawled. 'This is the way pirates do things!'

'My parents are going to be worried sick about me,' she warned him angrily.

Rogan shook his head. 'By the time they realise they need worry about you we'll be at the airport and you can call them and tell them you're all right. Graham too, if you feel you must,' he added harshly.

'Of course I feel I must,' she answered irritably. 'Saturday is our wedding-day, and—— The airport?' she realised suddenly, her eyes wide. 'Where are you taking me?' she demanded to know.

'Do you have some objection to flying?' Rogan frowned. 'I presumed you were flying to the Greek island you have chosen for your honeymoon.' He sighed. 'I suppose we could go by boat, but——'

'Go *where*?' She lost her temper.

'Still to an island, although I can't promise you the weather will be as hot,' he mocked.

'I take it this island has a name?' she demanded tautly.

'It does,' he confirmed lightly. 'We'll be staying at a friend's house,' he added cheerfully.

'*Where*?'

'I think your hair actually crackles with electricity when you get angry,' he mused.

'Rogan!' Her hands clenched into fists in her frustration.

'Wait and see,' he mocked infuriatingly. 'Do I take it I have your co-operation about flying over?'

Her mouth firmed. 'You don't have my *co-operation* in any of this,' she bit out, his use of the word suddenly striking her as odd. Unless ...? 'Maybe a nice long boat trip would be fun, after all,' she said slowly, watching his reaction. He actually paled!

'It will be a lot quicker if we fly,' he persuaded.

'Yes, but——'

'Caity, we're going by plane!' he told her decisively, his expression fierce.

She looked at him with glowing eyes, her mouth twitching with suppressed humour, humour she could no longer contain as she burst into husky laughter. 'I don't believe it,' she choked. 'A pirate who gets seasick!'

He looked uncomfortable. 'I'm glad you find it funny.' His tone implied the opposite.

She rested back against the head-rest, still chuckling. 'Another illusion shattered.' She shook her head, eyeing him mockingly.

'What illusion is that?' he growled.

'I could imagine you tied to the helm of your ship as the fierceness of the waves crashing over you rocked you so high you would have been washed overboard otherwise, the storm raging about you, tossing the ship about as if it were made of paper, while you—the captain—valiantly fought to keep it afloat. Surging up and down, up and—— I'm sorry, Rogan, did you say something?' She turned to him with widely enquiring eyes as he gave a weak moan.

He had gone grey at her vivid description! 'Couldn't you imagine I'd retired from the sea? I could still be the captain.'

'Hardly,' she derided. 'It just wouldn't be the same.' She shook her head regretfully, her eyes brimming over with laughter.

'I feel ill just at the thought of getting on anything that floats,' he admitted ruefully.

She gave an exaggerated sigh. 'Does that mean the waterbed is out too?'

'Give me a break!' He swallowed hard, seeming greyer than ever.

'Yet another illusion bites the dust,' she said melodramatically.

'I've abducted you before your wedding to another man, am even now in the process of carrying you off to my secret island, where I intend ravishing you until you beg for mercy; what more do you want?' Rogan looked pained.

'I don't know,' she said drily. 'This seems to be your fantasy, not mine!'

'All good pirates abduct their women, lock them in the cabin and have their wicked way with them as often as humanly possible,' he reasoned complainingly.

Caitlin's brows quirked with amusement. 'And how would you know that?'

He shrugged. 'I'm a black and white movie buff; Errol Flynn has always been my hero.'

'Because of his real life exploits, or because of his screen ones?' Caitlin mocked, having read—and thoroughly enjoyed—the film star's notorious life-story, and found it to be even more scandalous and daring than the film roles he played.

Rogan smiled appreciatively. 'Now he *was* a rogue!'

'And you aren't?' she jeered, relieved to notice they were actually approaching the airport now. The sooner she spoke to her parents and reassured them that she was all right the quicker their minds would be put at rest. Rogan was crazy, he had to be, and the wisest thing to do now was humour him.

'I'm not going to apologise for trying to save you from a marriage that would have been the biggest mistake of your life,' he told her arrogantly.

'And who gave you the right to make that decision for me?' she challenged icily.

'You did,' he reasoned confidently. 'The first time you kissed me.'

'Maybe I had a case of bride's last-minute jitters,'

she excused abruptly. 'You must know that you aren't my type at all.'

'No one has a *type*,' he dismissed scornfully. 'Attraction can flame between the ugliest of men and the most beautiful of women, and vice versa. There are no set rules to attraction. I can assure you I don't usually go for spoilt rich girls.'

'And I'm *never* attracted to arrogant bastards who think they rule the world!'

Silence followed her heated outburst, with Caitlin refusing even to acknowledge his presence beside her by so much as looking at him. What he had done, carrying her off in this way, was worse than arrogant, it was deliberately destructive, and she couldn't forgive him for the chaos he had caused, let alone feel a spark of the attraction she had felt towards him from the moment they met. He was selfish and manipulative, cared nothing for anyone's wishes but his own. But he would, *she* would make sure of that.

He parked her car in the airport long-term car-park, and they got a bus in to the terminal, Caitlin doing some quick working out as to where their destination could be by the terminal they went to.

'I wouldn't bother,' Rogan drawled as he saw her frown. 'I've chartered a plane to take us to where I want to go.'

She looked at him coolly. 'You have been busy this morning.'

'Haven't I?' His mouth twisted derisively.

'I could just stand here and scream.' She looked pointedly about the crowded terminal.

Rogan crossed his arms over his chest. 'Why don't you?' he challenged.

It would serve him right if she did exactly that! But she knew she wouldn't.

Amusement lightened her eyes. 'Maybe I'm just waiting to see what outrage you'll come out with next!'

'Well, at the moment I'm going to return the keys to the Jaguar to the desk and tell them where they can pick it up,' he drawled. 'And then you can make your telephone calls.'

'You're too kind,' she snapped sarcastically, her head back proudly.

'Not really,' he mocked. 'I'd hate your parents to become really worried and involve the police.'

'Of course,' she acknowledged drily.

'You know, you're taking this very well.' He looked at her consideringly. 'I didn't expect you to have hysterics or anything like that, you're much too controlled for that. But you're behaving much better than I'd hoped for.'

'Or planned?' she mocked.

He gave a slow smile at the taunt. 'I must admit I didn't have too much time to plan anything but getting you away from there.'

'I would never have guessed!' she drawled.

'You've been most co-operative,' he nodded.

And when he stopped congratulating himself long enough to ask why she had he might realise that she had wanted to be 'got away from there'! At the moment he just seemed triumphant in having succeeded this far, he didn't seem to have realised he couldn't have done it without her *full* co-operation. He had made so many mistakes, the main one being in bringing her to a public airport in this way!

She had realised last night that she had been making a mistake in marrying Graham, that fond of him as she was it wasn't enough, not when a man like Rogan could come along and set her alight with a mere touch. Maybe she would have admitted as much to him last night if he hadn't burst into her bedroom so arrogantly and demanded that she give up Graham!

She stood by their suitcases while Rogan paid for his hire car, anxious to make the calls home, knowing they were sure to be worried about her by now.

'Very good,' Rogan complimented her after she had spoken to her parents, telling them not to worry about her, that she was sorry about the chaos she had left them to face, that she needed a few days away to think about what she was doing with her life. They had just been relieved to hear that she was safe! 'I expected you to tell them the truth at any second,' Rogan added ruefully.

She had known that, it had been obvious from the tension he displayed every time she answered her parents' questions. 'What could I tell them?' she mocked. 'They would have thought I'd been drinking if I'd told them I'd been kidnapped by a seasick pirate!'

He laughed softly, kissing her with seductive gentleness. 'You have a very dry sense of humour!'

'Isn't that what we British are known for?' She was a little breathless from the touch of his lips. 'Stiff upper lip in the face of adversity, and all that?'

'There's nothing stiff about you,' he murmured before kissing her again.

'The same can't be said about you!' She drew back, trembling in spite of herself.

He shook his head reprovingly, the gleam in his eyes belying his expression. 'You're getting naughty now,' he rebuked.

Caitlin shrugged. 'Can I help it if you can't control yourself?'

'A lady wouldn't have drawn attention to my— er—condition,' he chided huskily.

'A *gentleman* wouldn't allow a lady to know about it,' she returned caustically.

'What am I supposed to do, pretend I don't want to take you here and now?' he bit out, his eyes narrowed.

'Well, as you aren't going to "take me here and now" that might be advisable!' She glared.

Rogan moved away from her with a sigh. 'Make your call to Graham,' he instructed curtly.

She frowned. 'Could I have a little privacy to talk to him?' Rogan stood so close to her in the supposedly sound-proof hood that he would be able to hear Graham's conversation as well as her own!

'What do you intend telling him?' He chewed thoughtfully on his inner lip.

Caitlin quirked auburn brows. 'That I might be a little late for the wedding! What do you think I'm going to tell him, Rogan?' she snapped angrily. 'I'm going to apologise for seemingly leaving him in the way I have,' she sighed.

'That's all?'

She tapped her foot impatiently on the floor. 'Isn't that enough?' she challenged. 'Don't you think I at least owe him that?'

'All right,' Rogan rasped. 'But make it quick, our plane is waiting for us.' He stepped out of the hood to wait several feet away.

It wasn't the ideal way she would have wished to talk to Graham, but she knew she couldn't make Rogan budge a step further away. At least he wouldn't be able to hear Graham's side of the conversation. It was some consolation.

'God, Caitlin,' snapped Graham as soon as her call was put through to him, 'what on earth do you mean by running away in this way?'

'I'm not running away.'

'It certainly seems like it!' he bit out.

She glanced awkwardly at Rogan, only to find him watching her intently. 'I'm sorry I didn't meet you this morning.'

'That doesn't matter,' he dismissed harshly. 'It's obvious we have nothing more to talk about.'

'It wasn't like that, Graham,' she muttered. 'I did intend meeting you this morning, I just——'

'Changed your mind before you got there,' he scorned. 'I suppose you realise you had us all worried out of our minds this morning before you called your parents just now and told them you were all right? We all thought you'd been involved in an accident or something,' he rebuked disgustedly.

'Where are you anyway? Your parents said it sounded like an airport.'

She hadn't thought of the fact that the noise, and the constant tannoy announcements of flights, would have carried down the line to her parents' worried ears. She doubted Rogan had realised that either. For such a self-confident man he was certainly bungling this. But at least this way she could be sure he had never done anything like this before!

'They were right,' she confirmed, smiling reassuringly at the scowling Rogan. 'I felt as if I needed to get completely away for a while. I'm sorry I've left you alone there to face everyone, but I—it couldn't be helped,' she added uncomfortably.

'I think you've been completely selfish and thoughtless,' he snapped. 'I suppose you really are sure this is what you want to do?' he added with a slight softening of his angry tone.

'I'm afraid so,' she said softly.

'I thought so,' he rasped. 'And when do you think you will have been "away" long enough?'

She glanced at Rogan as he shifted impatiently. 'I'm not sure,' she answered impatiently. 'I'll call you when I get home.' She rang off gently before he could issue any more well deserved insults.

Rogan watched her frowningly once they had boarded the aircraft he had chartered and the plane was taxiing for take-off. 'Was he angry?' Rogan finally bit out.

She gave him a scathing glance. 'What do you think?'

He shrugged. 'I think if you ran out on me only days before the wedding I would want to wring your beautiful little neck!'

And last night, when she had told Graham she couldn't marry him, that was exactly how he had felt!

# CHAPTER SIX

CAITLIN had watched Rogan leave with Gayle last night, and realised that, although Rogan wanted no more than an affair with her, she couldn't marry Graham feeling as she did about the other man. It wouldn't have been fair to him or their marriage.

Graham had been furious at her decision, as she had expected he would be, and their parents had been deeply shocked. She had persuaded him that it would save everyone embarrassment if they said they had mutually decided not to marry, although she had agreed to meet him in the morning to discuss how she felt after sleeping on her decision.

She hadn't realised then that Rogan would abduct her before she had time to tell Graham she still felt the same way. Rogan couldn't possibly realise that his arrogance had taken her away from an unpleasant situation just at the time she needed to get away. Although she would have left under less of a cloud if she had been given a choice!

She had no idea how deeply her feelings for Rogan went yet, although physically she couldn't deny him. And for a man who had 'tried marriage and didn't like it' he was behaving very strangely by carrying her off in this way. Maybe this time alone together would give them a chance to find out how they felt about each other, because, like the rest of her family, she was very much afraid she had met her love—and her match!—when she least expected to do so.

'You haven't said a word since we took off.' He watched her curiously.

'I'm sorry,' she returned sarcastically. 'I didn't realise I was here to provide your in-flight entertainment!'

He gave a deep sigh. 'You would have been bored as a wife within six months,' he dismissed confidently. 'Your life would have become a round of cocktail parties and charity committees.'

Caitlin looked at him derisively. 'I intended continuing with my career. And Graham hates cocktail parties!'

'Certain social obligations are necessary in his profession,' Rogan insisted.

'Graham's father always did all the socialising that was necessary for the company,' she informed him with saccharine sweetness.

A flush darkened his cheeks. 'His father will have to retire some time.'

'*I* love parties, Graham is the one who hates them,' she returned in a bored voice, almost able to hear Rogan's teeth gnashing together!

'You haven't asked me where we're going,' he bit out tightly.

'Not recently, no,' she acknowledged without interest.

'Well?' Rogan snapped after several minutes' silence when Caitlin just looked out of the window.

She looked up at him in feigned surprise,

knowing exactly how much she was annoying him. 'The Isle of Man, isn't it?' she stated calmly.

'How the hell did you——' He broke off forcefully, his eyes narrowed. 'What makes you think that?' His tone was deliberately casual.

She didn't think it at all, she *knew* it! Their flight path was unmistakable, and he had said an island. 'I'm sorry,' she shrugged. 'Perhaps I was wrong?'

'You aren't wrong,' he bit out.

'Oh, good,' she smiled happily. 'I love the Isle of Man.'

Rogan looked at her suspiciously. 'You've been there before?'

'A number of times,' she nodded. 'Daddy used to have friends who lived there several years ago. Which part are we going to?'

'Somewhere near a place called Ramsey.' He still scowled.

Caitlin nodded. 'It's prettier in the north of the island. The weather isn't quite as good, but the scenery compensates.'

'I was told it's only thirty miles long by ten miles wide,' Rogan frowned.

'It is,' she confirmed. 'But as it's in the Gulf Stream, and set between Ireland and England, the weather differs drastically from one end to the other. The south of the island is quite flat, whereas the north is quite mountainous, and so it can be sunny in the south when it's snowing in the north.'

'But not in September?' He sounded horrified at the idea.

'No.' She laughed at his expression. 'The heather

should be out now, deep purple, with pinks and orange.'

'This is just great.' He raised his eyes heaven-wards. 'I carry you off to an island and you know more about it than I do!'

Caitlin chuckled softly. 'You'll just have to face it, Rogan, you make a pretty poor pirate.'

'We haven't got as far as the ravishment yet,' he warned suggestively.

That wiped the amusement from her face; she was only too well aware of how successful he was at seduction. She also knew she couldn't give in to her own longings to capitulate, determined Rogan would feel more than desire for her before she allowed her own emotions full rein.

'Did I mention the wrong thing?' Rogan watched the play of emotions across her face.

'Oh no,' she scorned. 'I always discuss the prospect of having a complete stranger ravish me!'

His hand was gentle against her cheek. 'We've never been strangers, Caity,' he said huskily.

'You mean we know how to arouse each other!' she scorned.

'Not just that,' he frowned.

'Then what else?' she challenged. 'I know nothing about you but what you've chosen to tell me—and that isn't a lot!'

His face darkened. 'You mean you want to know if I had blond or dark hair as a baby, if I had freckles while I was growing up, if——'

'No!' she glared at him. 'I just want to know a little more about *you*.'

'The me you see today?' he taunted.

'Yes!' She gave an impatient frown at his mocking expression. 'And what made you the man that you are,' she added reluctantly.

'In other words, my life story?' Rogan scorned.

'Just the important bits,' she muttered resentfully.

He turned to stare sightlessly out of the window. 'When I was two years old my mother and father dumped me on my maiden aunt so that they could go off to seek their fame and fortune in the entertainment business without a kid hanging on to them; they fancied themselves as the Fred Astaire and Ginger Rogers of the time,' he rasped. 'They came back to see me for my birthday once a year. Only they somehow never quite made it for my birthday, they were always a few weeks out on the date,' he remembered bitterly. 'And as Christmas was always a busy time for them they were sure I would understand that although they wanted to be with me they couldn't. Sure I understood, a lot of people had parties that needed second-rate entertainment that time of year——'

'Rogan, please don't go on.'

'Why not?' he challenged. 'Isn't it pretty enough for you? No, of course it isn't,' he dismissed harshly. 'Well, it gets better! When I was six my father came back to New York; my mother chose to stay on in Las Vegas with the new "manager" she had found who was going to make her into a big star. I never saw her again. And without his Ginger my father didn't have any reason to do anything, and so my aunt supported both of us until I was old enough to pay our way. Only by then my aunt was dead.'

'Rogan, I'm sorry——'

'I sold her run-down house to buy an even more run-down apartment building,' he bit out. 'And when I had enough I bought another one, and then another one, until I finally owned half a dozen. And I never had to use any strong-arm tactics to get my rent either,' he added challengingly. 'I dealt fair with them and most of them dealt fair with me.' He had a closed expression on his face when he turned back to her. 'Now I own property all over the States, and I live in an apartment in Manhattan. But my dad died a drunk, and God knows what my mother was when she died! If you want to know anything else about me you'll have to look it up in the newspapers back home that seem to enjoy gossiping about my life!'

He had told her more than enough for her to realise what motivated him. Not only had his mother and father let him down, but also his wife, in a way he refused to talk about just now. And she knew enough about him to realise that he half-hated her for insisting he tell her at least part of what had made him the bitter and cynical man he was today.

'You forgot to mention that you're thinking of going into partnership with my father,' she teased.

His mouth twisted. 'Probably because it's still at the thinking stage,' he drawled. 'It's too big for either of us to take on alone, and yet neither of us is used to having a partner. I guess we'll reach a deal eventually.'

'You think so, after you abducted his daughter?' she derided.

'You seem more concerned with causing trouble between your father and myself than with what Graham would think were he to be told I've been with you during the "time you needed away"!' he scorned.

'That's because I'm sure Graham will forgive me when he knows the full circumstances.' Eventually! He had been very angry last night when she told him she couldn't marry him, but she had no doubt that he would eventually come around and realise she had only done it for the best.

Rogan's jaw clenched. 'I wouldn't,' he rasped.

'Because you aren't interested in marrying me, only in bedding me!'

The co-pilot cleared his throat awkwardly as he turned in his seat, the blush reaching the tips of his ears. 'We're about to land, Mr McCord,' he quickly informed them before hastily turning away again.

Caitlin kept her head bowed, knowing Rogan had to be furious with her as he too realised the two men had been able to overhear the whole of their conversation. And some of the things that had been said——!

'I think I'll use a different company for our trip back,' Rogan said ruefully once they stood inside the airport building surrounded by their cases, the two men having made their escape as quickly as was politely possible.

She grimaced. 'I completely forgot——'

'So did I—which is ridiculous when they were the

ones flying the plane!' he said self-disgustedly.

Having expected his anger to be directed towards her she was relieved to hear him take half the blame, looking about them expectantly.

Caitlin hadn't been to the island for several years, but nothing seemed to have changed too much. But then that was part of the island's charm and attraction to the many tourists who visited here each year, the quiet pace of life and the old-fashioned values. Her father always claimed that stepping on to the Isle of Man was like returning to the way England had been thirty years ago, and he meant it as a sincere compliment. The islanders lived their lives without the constant scramble that had made England such a rat-race in recent years. The people were friendly and courteous, never in a hurry, maintaining the values that made England seem noisy and overcrowded in comparison.

'What the hell is that?' Rogan came to a halt outside the automatic doors, the statue of the island's emblem, the three legs, standing in a garden opposite them. 'Don't tell me,' he shook his head. 'Let's just get the car and get going.'

He looked big and cramped in the small hatchback car that was all the hire firm had available, not liking the fact that he had to change the gears manually either.

Caitlin turned away to hide her smile, enjoying the drive. The island had the same lush greenery that was found in Ireland, probably because of its considerable rainfall, and the yellow gorse prevalent in hedgerows during the spring and summer had now given way to a carpet of purple heather.

Rogan was still frowning when she glanced at
him, although he brightened a little as they went
through the large town of Douglas, the island's
capital, glowering again when the signpost informed him that Ramsey was still fourteen miles
away.

Like the Channel Islands, the Isle of Man was a
tax haven, but in Caitlin's opinion it was by far the
prettier, as well as being larger than any of the
Channel Islands. As a young girl she had ridden
through the picturesque hills, taken long hikes up in
the mountains, and played on the beaches.

'Turn left here,' she hastily directed Rogan,
clinging to the door as he did so with a screech of
tyres. 'I know this is part of the TT course, but do
you have to drive like a maniac!' She glared at him,
rubbing her bruised arm.

'TT course?' he echoed, slowing down a little as
they left the town behind them to approach the
mountains.

'Race course,' she supplied absently, the heather
and pocket-green fields even more magnificent
from up here. 'Motorbikes,' she added as he still
looked puzzled.

'Here?' Now he looked astounded. 'But it's all so
quiet and peaceful!'

'Not during practice and race weeks it isn't,' she
smiled. 'It's a lot of fun, actually. Unless you
happen to live within the race-circuit, I expect!' she
grimaced.

Rogan looked as if he didn't quite believe her.

'They can't race bikes through these villages and towns!'

'But they do, over a hundred miles an hour most of the way,' she supplied with relish.

'That's insane!'

She shook her head. 'It's tradition. The race has been taking place here for over seventy years.'

He grimaced. 'Who am I to argue with tradition! These, I take it, are the mountains?'

'Yes. They——'

'What's that?' Rogan was gazing at the electric tram as it crossed the road in front of them.

Caitlin laughed happily. 'They also have horse-drawn trams on Douglas promenade during the summer months. And there's a steam-train down the south. And they aren't just there for show, they're part of the island's transportation.'

'It's incredible,' he said slowly as he moved the car onwards.

'I think it's unique,' she defended the favourite haunt of her youth.

'I didn't say I didn't like it.' Rogan shook his head a little dazedly. 'Those trams are a little like the cable cars we have in San Francisco.'

'Of course,' she nodded, a little mollified.

'I've never seen anywhere like this place before.' He gazed over the side of the road into the deep valley below.

Caitlin doubted he had ever before stayed anywhere like the thatched-roofed cottage that turned out to be their final destination either!

She loved it as it nestled enchantingly in the bay,

but from Rogan's expression he had obviously expected his friend's 'house' to be somewhat different from what it actually was.

A rose-garden fronted the cottage, a pathway leading down to the sea a short distance away as it pounded against the stones thrown ashore during rougher weather. It was a low building, painted pristine white, with black window-frames and doors, the thatched roof giving it a rustic charm that would look perfect with a puff of white smoke leaving the red chimney.

'It's lovely, Rogan.' She turned to him enthusiastically as he parked the car in the driveway.

'I was expecting something a little more—well——'

'Like the beautifully elegant houses we passed on the way here,' she supplied knowingly. 'I think this has much more character.'

'So did the old Chevy I had as a kid,' Rogan said drily, getting out of the car. 'But it was rarely out of the workshop,' he added as he opened the car door for her.

'Where's your appreciation for beauty?' She joined him. 'Look at the views!' she enthused, her eyes glowing bright blue as she looked from the grey-blue of the sea to the surrounding hills.

He gave a suppressed shiver. 'Why is it so much colder here than it was in London?'

'The sea-breezes, I expect,' she dismissed. 'Let's go and take a look inside.'

'Harry said the key's under the mat.' Rogan bent to retrieve it.

'How original,' she said drily as he unlocked the door.

They walked straight into a lounge with a wood-beamed ceiling, the room long and narrow, stairs near the door leading directly to the second level, a kitchen visible through an open doorway across from them.

'My God, it's colder inside than it is out,' Rogan shuddered as the chill pervaded his body. 'Where's the temperature switch for the heating?' He searched for the wall switch.

'Er—Rogan?' She stood with her hands behind her back as she watched him.

'Hmm?' He was preoccupied as he went through to the kitchen to look for the switch. 'There doesn't seem to be one,' he finally realised with a frown.

'No,' she acknowledged.

'Well, that's damn stupid,' he rasped. 'How do you control the heating?'

Her mouth quirked. 'Tell me, Rogan, have you lived in centrally heated homes all your life?'

'I guess so,' he nodded impatiently, obviously wondering what that had to do with anything.

'Then this should come as a new experience for you,' she said drily. 'If you want any heat I think you'll find the coal out at the back of the cottage, and the wood and paper to light it are in that bucket over there.'

Rogan gave the bucket next to the fireplace a startled look. 'I thought the fireplace was just for show,' he groaned. 'My God, it's only September, how can it be this cold?'

'My guess is that your friend hasn't been here for some time.' She ran her fingertips along the top of the coffee-table, collecting a layer of dust as she did so, as if to prove her point. 'And the thickness of the Manx-stone walls would keep it cool in here.'

'It isn't cool; it's like a damned ice-box!'

'It is a little chilly, I'll admit. But——'

'I'm freezing,' Rogan insisted. 'Come on,' he turned away, 'let's go and book into a hotel.'

She didn't want to stay in a hotel, this cottage would be much more conducive to their getting to know each other than being surrounded by a lot of strangers. 'A pirate who gets seasick *and* can't stand a little bit of cold?' she jeered.

He came to an abrupt halt, turning in the doorway to look at her. 'You can't really want to stay here?'

'All it needs is the cold of last winter aired out of it. You have to admit it's beautiful inside, Rogan.' She looked about them appreciatively, the cottage was decorated and furnished to fit in with the obvious age and mellowed charm of the place, the furniture looking like genuine antiques.

'Maybe I can answer that without bias when I stop turning blue!' he scowled.

Caitlin held back a smile with effort. 'You go and get our cases in from the car,' she took charge, 'and I'll light the fire.'

He turned, hesitating. 'Can you manage?'

She smiled. 'Better than you, I imagine. Go on, then you can get a sweater to put on until it warms up in here.'

'I'm not sure I brought one,' he grimaced.

'Then wear a jacket!' She crouched down to the task of lighting the fire.

By the time she had the fire blazing, the dryness of the paper and wood evidence that the cottage was only cold and not damp, Rogan had returned with their cases. She turned to him with a triumphant grin, the warmth of the flames already giving her cheeks a glow.

Rogan still looked disgruntled as he started to go up the stairs. 'Do you—— Hell!' He let out a yell as he knocked his head on a beam, dropping the cases to put a hand up to his temple with a pained grimace.

Caitlin quickly crossed the room to his side. 'Let me see if you've broken the skin.' She pushed his fingers away from the pained spot, probing gently. 'It's just bruised,' she realised with relief.

'*Just* bruised,' he repeated irritably. 'We can't stay in this cottage, Caity; I can't even stand up straight in parts of it!' he complained disgustedly, touching the tender lump that had already formed at the side of his head.

This time she actually had to bite her top lip to keep from laughing. He looked like a disgruntled little boy! 'What were you about to say before you bumped your head?' She opted for a safer subject.

'There are two bedrooms upstairs,' he scowled. 'Do you want to come up and choose which one you would like to use?'

At least, she had thought it was a safer subject! 'I

actually get to have my own room?' she derided
with raised brows.

'Well, if you would rather not——'

'I would,' she cut in hastily at his wolfish grin.
'But what happened to having your wicked way
with me as often as humanly possible?'

'No need to sound disappointed, Caity,' he
mocked. 'I'm sure that can still be arranged. I just
thought you might prefer to have your own
bedroom for the time in between ravishments.'

'There's no need to act so smug just because I'm
surprised you've managed to show some sign of
human decency,' she snapped, stung that he had
taken her surprise as a sign of encouragement.

'Careful, Caity,' he warned softly. 'I could always
change my mind about the separate rooms.'

'You might also, with a little practice,' she
scorned, 'learn how to keep the fire burning all
night, and work out how we get our supply of hot
water!'

'There's no hot water?' he groaned. 'And I was
just thinking a hot bath might help thaw me out!'

'You certainly weren't a Boy Scout, were you?'
she derided, preceding him up the stairs, the
moment of danger passed. Only the moment.

His only reply was a grunt as he staggered up the
stairway behind her with her two big suitcases.

There were two bedrooms, both of them small,
Rogan almost bent double as he avoided the sloping
beamed ceilings. One of the rooms was decorated in
pink, the other one lemon, and out of respect for his
male ego—that had already taken quite a beating

today!—Caitlin chose the pink one. There was also a bathroom between the two rooms, which they obviously had to share.

Rogan dropped her cases down on the single bed, looking around the small room with a grimace. 'Are you sure you're going to have room to put all your things? The other room is slightly larger——'

'I couldn't put you through the humiliation of sleeping in a pink room,' she derided as she turned from admiring the view out to sea from her bedroom window, several small fishing boats visible in the distance.

'Who says I would be sleeping here?' he challenged softly.

'I do,' she told him firmly. 'Let's get some rules clear right from the start, Rogan,' she bit out tautly. 'I may have been given no choice about being brought here, but now that I am here *I'll* decide when and where I'll go to bed with you. And *if* I will,' she added forcefully. 'Which is still debatable.'

Rogan raised mocking brows. 'Which one of us was abducted?' he drawled.

The enormity of the gamble she was taking washed over her. She had told Graham she couldn't marry him, had hurt and disappointed her parents, especially her mother, and all because of a man she knew didn't love her.

His humour faded to be replaced by a frown as he saw her sudden anguish. 'Caity, what is it?'

She avoided his reaching hands. 'Could I have a few minutes to myself?' she requested abruptly. 'I need time to—to think.'

'Would you like to talk?'

'I just want to be alone!' she told him tensely.

'Of course.' He still looked worried. 'Caity, I never meant to hurt you,' he told her anxiously.

Just as she hadn't meant to hurt anyone either, not Graham, not her parents, but this man had invaded her life with the force of a tidal wave, and she was still floundering in his wake. She needed time alone to regain her feet.

She nodded. 'I'll be down soon.'

'You're sure there's nothing I can do?' He watched her closely.

'Nothing,' she bit out dismissively.

He seemed about to say something else, and then thought better of it, his feet sounding noisily on the stairs as he went slowly down them.

Caitlin sat down heavily in the bedroom chair, fighting back the tears, losing the battle as they cascaded down her cheeks. She didn't like to cry, she hated the way it made her feel, but at this moment she needed the emotional release.

Saturday should have been her wedding-day, she should have become *Graham's* wife in three days' time. Instead she was miles away from home, in a cottage that looked as if it had only recently been introduced to indoor plumbing, with a man she had just realised she was in love with.

She had thought she had merely been using his abduction of her as a convenient way to get away from all the chaos at home, but the things he had told her about himself on the flight over here, his

# . . . be tempted!

See inside for special
4 FREE BOOKS offer

**Harlequin Presents**®

# Discover deliciously different romance with 4 Free Novels from

## *Harlequin Presents*

Sit back and enjoy four exciting romances—yours **FREE** from Harlequin Reader Service! But wait . . . there's *even more* to this great offer!

**HARLEQUIN FOLDING UMBRELLA— ABSOLUTELY FREE!** You'll love your Harlequin umbrella. Its bright color will cheer you up on even the gloomiest day. It's made of rugged nylon to last for years, and is so compact (folds to 15″) you can carry it in your purse or briefcase. This folding umbrella is yours free with this offer!

**PLUS A FREE MYSTERY GIFT**—a surprise bonus that will delight you!

All this just for trying our Reader Service!

**MONEY-SAVING HOME DELIVERY!**

Once you receive your 4 FREE books and gifts, you'll be able to preview more great romance reading in the convenience of your own home at less than retail prices. Every month we'll deliver 8 brand-new Harlequin Presents novels right to your door months before they appear in stores. If you decide to keep them, they'll be yours for only $2.24 each! That's .26¢ less per book than what you pay in stores—plus .89¢ postage and handling per shipment.

**BE TEMPTED! COMPLETE, DETACH AND MAIL YOUR POSTPAID ORDER CARD TODAY AND RECEIVE 4 FREE BOOKS, A FOLDING UMBRELLA AND MYSTERY GIFT—PLUS LOTS MORE!**

# A FREE
# Folding Umbrella
*and* Mystery Gift *await you, too!*

## HARLEQUIN READER SERVICE "NO-RISK" GUARANTEE

- There's no obligation to buy—and the free books and gifts remain yours to keep.
- You pay the lowest price possible and receive books before they appear in stores.
- You may end your subscription anytime—just write and let us know.

If offer card is missing, write to: Harlequin Reader Service, P.O. Box 609, Fort Erie, Ontario, L2A 5X3

Clip and mail this postpaid card today!

**Business Reply Mail**

No Postage Stamp
Necessary if Mailed
in Canada

Postage will be paid by

**Harlequin Reader Service**
P.O. Box 609
Fort Erie, Ontario
L2A 9Z9

Canada Post
Postes Canada
125

endearing behaviour since they had arrived, had only served to show her she *was* the one who was in trouble. She was in love with a man who had been so badly scarred by life and his marriage that he didn't even believe in the emotion!

# CHAPTER SEVEN

'FOOD?'

'Hmm?' Rogan stood in front of the blazing fire, having found a sweater in one of his cases, its dark green colour suiting him perfectly, although he didn't seem to be any warmer.

'Or were you expecting us to live on love alone?' Caitlin mocked, completing her descent down the stairs, in control again now, no trace of the tears she had recently shed on her perfectly made-up face.

'We could try,' he invited throatily.

She shook her head. 'I happen to be hungry for food. Do we have any?'

'I thought we could go shopping for some now we're here,' he shrugged.

Caitlin gave a brittle smile. 'This is to be an open imprisonment, then,' she derided.

His mouth tightened. 'You aren't a prisoner, Caity,' he rasped.

'Then what am I doing in this cottage with a man I don't know?' Her voice cracked with tension.

'It's because you don't know me very well that I suggested we have separate bedrooms—for now,' he added gratingly. 'But if the only way to show you that you *want* to be with me is to take you to bed right now then I'll do it!' His eyes glittered dangerously.

He meant it. She didn't *need* to know him well to realise that! Her head went back in challenge. 'I told you I would let you know if and when.'

Gold flames sparkled in emerald depths, although Rogan quickly had himself under control again. 'Today has been difficult for you,' he bit out. 'So I'm going to overlook——'

'Don't do me any favours,' she told him tautly.

'Caity——'

'And stop calling me that!' she shouted, mortified as the tears began to fall again.

'God, Caity, don't cry!' Rogan moved towards her. 'Anything but that!' His arms closed about her.

Her first instinct was to fight, hitting out at him with her fists, until his mouth closed possessively over hers, and then her passion all went into returning that kiss, his lips firm and yet softly enticing as he held her fiercely against him.

Her defences collapsed completely, begging for his gentleness, sobbing in her throat as his arms relaxed their vice-like grip about her waist, his lips sensuously persuasive against hers.

'Caity, I'm sorry.' He rested his forehead damply against hers. 'I didn't mean to make you cry.'

She berated herself for her weakness, moving determinedly out of his arms. 'Now you see what happens when you forget to feed me!' She straightened her sweater over her skirt. 'I haven't had anything to eat since dinner last night.'

Rogan seemed relieved at this offered explanation for her breakdown, even if he didn't totally believe it. 'As you're the one who knows the island you may as well drive us to the shops.'

Caitlin's spirits rose during the short drive into Ramsey; she felt as if she were visiting an old friend, parking in St Paul's Square, the two of them arguing over what food to buy once they got into the supermarket, Caitlin choosing salad stuff, Rogan insisting he wanted hot meals. In the end they compromised, choosing salad to act as side-dishes to the hot food.

'Where to now?' Rogan straightened after placing the boxes of groceries in the boot of the car.

'I want to choose a book to read from the shop over there,' she pointed.

'Expecting your evenings to be boring and empty, are you?' Rogan drawled mockingly.

She looked at him in challenge. 'You mean they won't be? The cottage has no television, you know,' she reminded him. 'And I didn't have the chance to pack any reading material!'

His lids lowered sensuously over deep green eyes. 'I can think of something that will keep us entertained for hours,' he told her throatily.

The blush was unexpected, and she looked about them uncomfortably. 'Behave yourself!' she hissed.

He looked hurt by the rebuke. 'I was talking about Trivial Pursuit, of course.' He sounded affronted that she could have imagined he meant anything else!

Caitlin frowned. 'You mean that board-game they keep advertising on television?'

'Do they?' He looked interested. 'A couple of friends and I have formed our own club at home.'

'If it's anything like Monopoly——'

'It isn't,' he assured her hastily. 'You can't be knocked out of this game. And the questions are mainly general knowledge, even if they are on specific subjects.'

He looked so eager that she didn't have the heart to tell him she didn't like board-games very much, always losing to her brother when they were younger.

In the end they bought the board-game and the book, although Rogan assured her she wouldn't need the latter now that they had the Trivial Pursuit. He set the game up in the lounge while she prepared them some lunch with the crusty French stick and soup they had bought.

It was one thing to decide to keep him at arms' length until they were more sure of their feelings for each other, quite another to have to compete for his attention with a board-game!

'Oh no!' came his sudden cry from the lounge as Caitlin was stirring the warming soup.

She dropped the spoon with a clatter, uncaring of the fact that she had splattered soup all over the powder-blue jumper she wore, and rushed into the lounge.

Rogan was sitting on the sofa bending over the coffee-table where he had set up the board-game, looking up at her with a pained expression.

'What is it?' she demanded. 'Have you hurt yourself?' She frowned her concern.

He groaned. 'The questions have been altered to suit the English market!'

Her eyes widened as she took in the full significance of what he was saying. 'Does that mean you aren't hurt?' she prompted softly.

'Hurt?' he repeated irritably.

'As in seriously injured,' she nodded impatiently.

'Of course not,' he dismissed, frowning down at the card he held containing the questions that had so upset him.

'You just called out that way because the questions are English rather than American, as you expected?' she clarified.

'Didn't I just say that? I don't—— Caity, what are you doing?' he cried as she picked up the board, dropping the dice and other pieces on to the carpeted floor as she did so. 'Caity!' he warned just as she hit him over the head with the board. 'What did you do that for?' he muttered as he rubbed the injured spot.

She threw the board down disgustedly, giving him a saccharin-sweet smile. 'Shall we start with the fact that because I thought you had seriously injured yourself in some way I rushed in here in such a panic that I've splashed soup all over my jumper and ruined it? Added to that you almost gave me a heart-attack calling out in that way! And shall we end with the fact that *the soup is burning*?' she asked before dashing back into the kitchen.

The soup had actually come to a boil, bubbled up and gone over the top of the saucepan, was even now burning black on the hob-plate.

She snatched the saucepan off the hob, dropping it into the sink, and the smell of the burning liquid on the hob filled the room.

'Why didn't you just tell me you can't cook?' Rogan drawled from the open doorway, backing up as Caitlin advanced on him threateningly, her eyes blazing. 'Now, now, Caity,' he held up her hands to ward her off. 'I was only teasing.'

'They would never imprison me for killing my abductor!' she muttered.

'You've already beaten me over the head in the exact spot I was injured earlier,' he complained.

'You weren't injured, you walked into the ceiling,' she scorned.

'It still hurts,' he said in a disgruntled voice.

'Good,' Caitlin told him with satisfaction, walking straight past him and up the stairs, leaning over the rail to call down to him. 'If you want soup with your lunch it's in the tin in the cupboard, and the tin-opener is in the drawer.'

She slipped off the splattered jumper, sponging it and leaving it in the bathroom to dry before donning another one in a shade of green that reminded her of Rogan's eyes. She wouldn't have worn it for that very reason, but unfortunately Rogan had only packed two jumpers for her when he had rifled through her cupboards and drawers at home.

He hadn't found time to unpack either, she realised as she passed his bedroom door; his cases lay open on his bed.

'Lunch is ready,' he called up the stairs just as she was about to give in to the temptation of reaching out and touching the rumpled clothing.

She pulled her hand away as if she had been burnt, and hurried down the stairs.

Typically the soup that Rogan had warmed through proved to be exactly that, not boiled or burnt, but perfectly warmed. Caitlin consoled herself with the fact that she had filled the delicious French stick with cheese. Maybe that wasn't such a great feat, she acknowledged, but the coffee she had made was excellent, even Rogan said so.

'Let's leave those until later,' he suggested once they had stacked the dishes in the kitchen. 'I thought we could go exploring now.'

'But I thought you wanted to play the game.'

'I do. And we will,' he added throatily. 'But there's no rush. We have time.'

Caitlin ignored his double meaning. 'You're just afraid you'll lose because the questions aren't all American,' she taunted as she pulled on her cream-coloured jacket.

'We'll see who loses,' he challenged. 'Later.'

She wished she didn't have the feeling he was still talking about a different game from the one she was discussing!

Their cove consisted mainly of a pebble beach, but there was a trodden pathway going along the steep hills either side, and they set off towards the north of the island, walking single file as the pathway wasn't wide enough for anything else.

Caitlin felt the best she had all day as the breeze blew all the cobwebs away, giving her an exhilarated feeling. The view across to England and Scotland was spectacular, the mountains clearly visible across the miles and miles of sea.

'Not feeling seasick?' she mocked when they decided to turn around.

Rogan gave her a censorious look. 'It's only when I get on a boat that it happens, not just looking at it.'

'Oh,' she nodded mockingly, her hair whipped about her face by the wind.

'If you don't behave the cook amongst us won't offer to make dinner,' he drawled.

'Warming a can of soup doesn't make you a cook!' She walked behind him, picking her way carefully; the going was steep and slippery in places, and she was glad she had some flat shoes with her, although they were more suited to the sightseeing she had expected to do with Graham in Greece when she had bought them a couple of weeks ago.

'It makes me a better one than you to date,' Rogan told her softly.

She couldn't dispute that, imagining all the things she would like to do to him to cause him injury as they continued back to the cottage. How could he be so infuriating and yet so irresistible at the same time? Maybe if she had been able to answer that, she and Graham would have been married on Saturday after all.

'What does he use it for?' she asked suddenly.

'Hmm?' Rogan queried without turning around.

'The cottage,' she explained with a frown. 'It obviously isn't your friend's main residence, so what does he use it for?'

He paused to look at her beneath raised brows.

'Pretty much the same as us, I imagine,' he drawled.

'You mean you have a friend who kidnaps brides too?' She shook her head reprovingly.

'Only his own bride,' Rogan drawled. 'He's been happily married for twenty years!'

'I see. Then I suppose the cottage must be a holiday—— Oh, look!' she cried excitedly.

Her cry took Rogan so much by surprise that his feet went from under him and he landed with a thump on the muddy pathway.

'What is it?' he looked up at her anxiously. 'What happened?' He stood up, wiping his muddy hands on the sides of his denims. 'Are you hurt?'

'No. I—I was just pointing out the seals,' she explained reluctantly.

Rogan had been inspecting the damage done to the seat of his trousers, slowly turning to face her at her denial. 'Seals?' he repeated in a dangerously soft voice.

Colour darkened the rose of her cheeks. 'Yes— seals,' she confirmed with a grimace. 'You know, those things that swim in the sea and eat fish.'

'I know what they are, Caity,' he told her gruffly. 'I just didn't expect to have almost broken my neck over them!'

'You didn't land anywhere near your neck!' she taunted, the drying mud on the seat of his denims evidence of that.

'You're right,' he rasped. 'I could have damaged something much more valuable than my neck!'

Caitlin looked away. 'Do you want to see the seals or not?'

He moved to her side, squinting his eyes against the glare on the water. 'Where?'

'Over there.' She pointed to the bobbing dark grey head in the bay. 'And there.' She pointed to another one. 'Aren't they lovely!' Her eyes glowed.

'Lovely.'

She tensed at his husky tone, looking up at him nervously. His eyes had darkened, gone sensuously warm as he gazed right back at her. Caitlin looked away again quickly. 'We'll have to take a drive over to Blue Point one day,' she hurried into speech, 'you can see a dozen or more of them over there. They——'

'Caity.'

Her breath quickened at his husky groan. 'They almost come up on to the beach,' she continued breathlessly.

'Caity!'

She swallowed hard, breathing becoming almost impossible. 'I find it fascinating that they——'

'*Caity!*' he sighed her name forcefully as he put his arms about her. 'Kiss me!'

'I——'

'Show me you aren't the child you look to me right now,' he groaned.

Child? *Child*! If he wanted proof she was a woman he was going to get it!

Her arms curved about his neck as she arched up into him, wool against wool, denim against denim, flesh against flesh as she moved her mouth provocatively against and across his.

His chest moved raggedly against hers as the tip

of her tongue darted experimentally into his mouth, engaging in battle with his, finally retreating, only to be followed as he invaded her, searching out the pleasure spots with sensual accuracy.

As the wind blew about them Rogan's hand sought, and found, entry to her jumper, moving beneath the wool to caress her breasts through the silky camisole, the nipples hardening pleasurably.

It was the cry of a gull that broke them apart, Rogan looking down at her with dazed eyes as his hand still rested possessively against one of her breasts, his breathing ragged as he fought for control.

'You convinced me,' he rasped finally. 'You're a woman in every sense of the word!'

'And don't forget it again!' Caitlin bit out tautly, shaking a little as she walked off to take the lead the rest of the way back.

She walked briskly, breathing deeply in an effort to calm her own leaping senses. She knew she had been goaded into kissing him the way she had, but she could no sooner have resisted the challenge than she could decide never to see him again. She would just have to be more careful when around Mr Rogan McCord!

They paused on the beach to watch the two seals as they disappeared beneath the waves to search for fish only to bob up again a second later in another spot.

'I'm sure they know we're watching them,' Caitlin smiled at their antics.

Rogan nodded. 'They're great showmen.' He

turned to her with mocking eyes. 'Ready to be beaten at Trivial Pursuit?'

Another challenge. But she didn't in the least mind meeting this one!

The game was exactly what Rogan had said it was, a case of answering general knowledge questions about specific subjects, and you either knew the answer or you didn't, there was no subterfuge involved. Caitlin loved it when Rogan landed on a sport question; he knew absolutely nothing about English sport! Not that she was much better on that subject, but some of the answers Rogan gave were hilarious, although on most other subjects he was quite well informed.

She finally conceded that he was the winner, amazed to see that they had actually been playing for over two hours.

Rogan stretched stiffly. 'I'll go and cook a couple of steaks for dinner.' He stood up.

'I'll help you——'

'Relax, Caity,' he insisted. 'I grill a pretty good steak.'

'I could get the salads ready for you,' she offered lightly.

'I don't think the kitchen is big enough for both of us to work in there without my blood pressure shooting through the ceiling,' he said drily. 'Why don't you just sit here and watch the fire?'

She shook her head. 'I think I'll go and do my unpacking.' She stood up decisively. 'Mind your——' She gave a rueful grimace as her warning came too late and he hit his head on the top of the doorway into the kitchen.

'I think I'm going to walk around with a permanent lump on my head.' He gingerly touched the sore spot. 'And no wisecracks from you, young lady!' he warned as mischievous laughter gleamed in her eyes.

Her eyes glowed like twin sapphires. 'My lips are sealed,' she assured him lightly.

His brows arched. 'Not permanently, I hope,' he drawled mockingly.

Caitlin gave him a reproving look before going up the stairs.

Most of her clothes, she realised as she unpacked them, were unsuitable for the island, but at least Rogan had thought to put in a couple of jumpers and pairs of trousers.

The frothy white nightgown she had looked at only that morning seemed to mock her as it lay on top of the second case; the beautiful white creation had been a gift from her mother to wear for her bridegroom on their wedding-night. She wondered if Rogan had realised that when he packed it, and then decided he probably hadn't; he wouldn't want anything to remind her of her bridegroom when she was with him.

He still hadn't called her down for dinner by the time she had unpacked all her clothes into the drawers and small wardrobe, and arranged her toiletries in the bathroom, and so she hesitated as she was about to pass his bedroom, his cases still lying open untidily on the bed.

Why not; he wasn't going to find the time to do it

himself in the next few hours, and she had nothing else to do.

His clothes, she had noticed, were all of the finest quality, tailored trousers and suits, silk shirts, his shoes hand-made. All signs of his success, if his arrogance weren't already proof of that.

He travelled light for a man moving from country to country on business, even his toiletries were kept to the minimum. Feeling slightly ridiculous for the weakness, Caitlin allowed herself the luxury of breathing deeply of the elusive aftershave he wore, smiling as she envisaged his toiletries standing in the bathroom cabinet beside hers. There was something very intimate about the thought.

Finally she couldn't resist the impulse, lining the things across from hers in the cabinet. They looked too intimate; if Rogan ever saw them like that he would probably pack up both their things and take her back to London.

She wanted him to fall in love with her, not send him running away from her!

# CHAPTER EIGHT

'DELICIOUS!' Caitlin sat back replete after eating the meal Rogan had prepared for them. He hadn't been exaggerating when he claimed he 'grilled a pretty good steak'! He had also made a tasty dressing to go with the salad.

'Thank you,' he mocked.

'Do you have much opportunity to cook when you're at home?' she asked interestedly, sipping her wine.

'Or do I eat out at restaurants all the time?' he drawled derisively, sitting across the small dining-table from her as it stood at one end of the long lounge. 'Occasionally I prepare a quiet dinner for two at my apartment,' he drawled throatily.

Caitlin ruefully admitted she had walked into that with her eyes open! 'That wasn't the sort of "cooking" I meant!'

Rogan grinned. 'No?'

She stood up abruptly, no longer wanting to know about the other women who had been in his life, not when they had also helped form his cynicism towards all women. 'I'll clear away now. I thought I'd take a bath afterwards,' she added impulsively.

'Good idea.' He moved to help her. 'It will help relax you.'

Caitlin gave him a sharp look. The discovery that

she loved this man meant this abduction was no longer amusing.

'I wasn't aware that I needed to relax,' she bit out, the plates rattling as she almost slammed them into the sink, the water hissing on them as she turned on the taps.

'You're very taut. You see,' mocked Rogan as she gave a start as his hands fell lightly on to her shoulders, 'I have the perfect thing to relax you,' he murmured throatily.

Caitlin easily slipped out from beneath his hands. 'I would say you're far from perfect,' she derided.

He feigned hurt surprise. 'I was thinking of another game of Trivial Pursuit, of course,' he taunted.

She could feel the heat in her cheeks, and wondered how she was supposed to maintain her dignity when he kept making a fool of her so easily. 'You really are addicted to the game, aren't you?' she scorned.

Rogan shrugged. 'There's something else I'm much more addicted to, but I don't think you're in the mood for that right now.'

This time Caitlin didn't blush. 'I'm not in the mood to be beaten at that stupid game again, either!'

He looked disappointed by her refusal. 'You wouldn't feel that way about it if you just played it a couple more times.'

How could she resist a thirty-six-year-old man who somehow managed to look as hurt as a child thirty years younger might have done by her refusal to play with him! 'All right,' she sighed. 'Just let me clear away here.' She looked pointedly at the untidy clutter of the kitchen. 'The master chef seems to have made a terrible mess!'

He held up his hands defensively. 'I never claimed to be a tidy cook.'

'I think that's just as well,' she taunted as she began to put things back in the cupboards.

To an outsider the two of them sitting down to play the board-game in front of a roaring fire would have looked very homely. But as Caitlin found it more and more difficult to concentrate on the questions being asked, let alone to think of the right answers, she knew she was far from relaxed.

Rogan played as well as he had that afternoon, but there was a tension about him too that didn't sit naturally on his shoulders.

'Why don't you go up and have your bath?' he suggested when she gave a fourth wrong answer in a row.

'And give you the game, I suppose?' she shot back.

He grinned. 'Well, of course!'

'All right,' she sighed, standing up. 'Can I leave you to clear away down here?'

He gave her a mocking look. 'There really isn't that much to do.'

'No,' she acknowledged slowly. 'But don't forget to put more coal on the fire before you come to bed, and there's a guard to stand in front of it, and——'

'Go, Caity!' he ordered forcefully. 'I may be new to this, but I'm sure I can manage.'

She was sure he could too. If he had managed to amass a fortune from buying one run-down apartment building he could certainly manage to cope with this small cottage!

She added a liberal amount of her favourite Chlöe to her steaming bath water before luxuriating back in the scented warmth, opening the book she had bought that day, soon losing herself in the story.

The water had cooled a couple of times and been reheated again by the time Rogan knocked on the bathroom door a couple of hours later.

She looked up with a frown at the interruption. 'What is it?'

'It's almost midnight, you've been in there nearly two hours!'

'So?'

'So isn't it time you got out?' He sounded exasperated.

'I'm sorry, you should have said earlier if you wanted to use the bathroom——'

'I don't,' he cut in impatiently. 'I just thought that——'

'Thought what?' Caitlin was more puzzled than ever, her brow clearing suddenly, her expression one of anger. 'Rogan, tonight is definitely *not* the time or place for this!'

He sighed. 'I wasn't suggesting it was.'

'No?' she scorned, knowing that was exactly what he *had* thought!

'No!' he rasped back. 'God, you've been in there so long you probably look like a wrinkled prune!'

She looked down at the creamy length of her

body. 'I don't think I look in the least like a prune, Rogan,' she told him throatily. 'More like—Rogan? Rogan, are you there?' she queried softly, the silence outside the door ominous. He had gone!

She quickly got out of the bath, towelling herself dry before pulling on the white nightgown and matching robe she had brought into the room with her, releasing her hair from the ribbon on the crown of her head.

'Rogan, you——' His bedroom was empty, although the rumpled bedclothes were evidence he had been lying on top of them at some time during the last two hours. 'Rogan, you——' The lounge was empty too, and she frowned her puzzlement. Where could he have gone?

There weren't too many places he could be in this tiny cottage, and she had exhausted her search in five minutes, going to the door to step outside. She spotted him in seconds, standing on the shoreline, looking out over the moonlit sea.

'Rogan?' she called to him worriedly as he stood so still, the crash of the waves against the pebbles preventing him from hearing her. 'Rogan?' She picked her way carefully across the stones, her flimsy slippers completely inadequate on the uneven ground.

'What the hell——!' He had turned and seen her, his eyes gleaming in the moonlight as he stared at her ghostly appearance, her hair like a shimmering red flame against the whiteness of the floaty material. 'My God, Caity,' he said slowly. 'You look—pagan,' he groaned.

She swallowed hard at the naked passion in his eyes. 'I—I'm sorry about just now,' she said breathlessly. 'I didn't mean to hog the bathroom. Everyone at home knows that when I say I'm going to have a bath it really means I'm going to read a book in the bath. I shower if all I want to do is wash.'

'I didn't realise.' His gaze still burnt across her.

'No. I—— What are you doing out here?' The wind was cold and icy, easily piercing her sheer clothing.

'Trying to resist the urge to go into the bathroom, lift you out of the scented water that's been driving me crazy the last two hours, and carry you to my bed!' he admitted with a groan.

'Oh,' she gasped, breathing raggedly.

'Is that all you have to say?' Rogan withdrew his clenched fists from his trouser pockets. 'Caity, I want you until I can't think of anything else.'

It was madness, absolute madness when she had known him a total of three days, but she wanted him too! Quite shamelessly.

'—I can't take you,' she heard him say, her eyes widening with shock as she took in the full impact of the words. He sighed. 'Standing here gave me time to think, and it's made me realise exactly what I've done. The two of us have been playing games ever since we met, but today I went too far.' He shook his head. 'Call it a brainstorm, whatever, but I'm over it now. And tomorrow I'm taking you back so that you can marry Graham as planned.'

'You can't do that!' she gasped.

'You said he would understand your need to get away.'

'Well, he will,' she nodded. 'But——'

'I've been selfish, sweetheart,' he rasped, his jaw clenched. 'I don't believe you and Graham are right for each other, but why should I expect you to give all that up for an affair with me?'

If they went back now he would know she had been deceiving him today, that there was no Graham to go back to! And after that she would probably never see him again!

'Rogan——' Her stumble was completely unexpected, as was the jarring pain in her knee as it made contact with a particularly large stone.

'Caity?' Rogan was instantly kneeling beside her. 'Sweetheart!' he groaned as she looked up at him with tear-drenched eyes. 'God, I must have been insane to have brought you here!' He pulled her to her feet in front of him, frowning darkly as she shivered. 'You're freezing,' he realised self-disgust-edly, his arms going about her. 'Let's go back inside.'

'Rogan,' she halted him, 'I can't go back now; what would I tell everyone? What could I say to explain why I disappeared in the first place?'

'I'd do it for you if I could, Caity.' He kept her held against him as they hurried back to the welcoming cottage. 'But my presence could only make the situation worse.'

It couldn't be any worse. And she didn't want to go back. Not yet. She had been hoping that by the time they left here they could go back and tell her family that *they* were getting married.

'My knee really does hurt,' she groaned once they were inside the cottage, watching him from beneath lowered lashes as he carefully set her down on the sofa before examining her leg.

'Mm, it looks bruised.' Rogan bent over her, his fingers gentle against her skin, the glow from the fire giving his hair a blue-black sheen.

Caitlin watched him with enjoyment. There was something very right about his hands on her flesh, as if they had always belonged there. Which she felt sure they had. It might not have been love at first sight for her, but it certainly had been the second time she saw him.

'Still hurt?' Rogan frowned as he saw the pain in her eyes.

'Yes. Yes, it does,' she confirmed weakly. 'Would you mind helping me up the stairs?'

He looked doubtful about the width of the stairs being able to take them both but nodded anyway.

'Mind your——' She smiled as he remembered to duck in time. 'A few more days' practice and you should avoid knocking your head altogether!'

'We're going back tomorrow,' Rogan told her grimly. 'I'll deliver you back to your home, and then leave you and Graham to get on with your happy-ever-after.'

Caitlin watched him curiously as he sat her on the side of the bed to remove her slippers. 'Why did your marriage fail?' she finally asked softly, knowing by the way he stiffened that it wasn't a subject he cared to discuss with anyone.

'I don't remember saying it failed,' he rasped. 'I said I'd tried it and I didn't like it.'

'Yes. But——'

'Caity,' the fury in glittering green eyes silenced her, 'I don't like talking about it either!'

'But there has to be a reason——'

'There is,' he grated. 'But it's none of your damned business, is it?'

She bit painfully on her bottom lip. 'No—I suppose not.'

'Definitely not.' He straightened. 'Now get some sleep, we'll be leaving in the morning.'

'Rogan ...?'

He turned at the door. 'What is it?'

Gone was the arrogant tease she had known until now, and in his place was a cold stranger. And she didn't know if it were the fact that they were going back or the mention of his marriage that had done it. She had a feeling it was a combination of the two.

'I—aren't you staying with me tonight?' She blushed at having to be the one to ask him.

His eyes became almost black, his expression unreadable. 'You're Graham's bride, not mine,' he bit out.

'Yes. But——'

'Caitlin, I have my doubts about your fall outside being an accident, and I don't particularly care what games you played before and after you met Graham; it's up to him to keep you under control once you're married. But I have no intention of making love to you tonight or any other night.'

Her eyes blazed. 'You hypocritical——'

'Careful,' he told her icily. 'I can't stand to hear a woman swear.'

'Bastard!' she finished with satisfaction, angry colour aflame in her cheeks. 'You brought me here for the sole purpose *of* making love to me,' she accused heatedly.

'Yes,' he admitted heavily. 'It was a mistake. I should have realised that, the moment you asked me if *I* intended marrying you!'

'I was joking at the time,' she gasped. 'Scornful, if I remember correctly.'

'Nevertheless, you would have accepted if I'd said yes,' he grated.

'Get out of here, you—you——' She picked up a pillow and threw it at him.

'Pirate?' he taunted as the pillow hit him ineffectually in the chest before sliding to the floor.

'Yes!' She glared at him.

Rogan gave a humourless smile. 'That was exactly what I intended to be with you after you called me one that first evening. But tonight, as I waited for you to get out of the bath, I remembered that Pat—my wife—used to read that type of historical romance. I also realised something else,' he added grimly.

'And what was that?' Caitlin snapped her lack of interest in anything he had realised.

'No matter how awful those men were to the heroine, no matter how brutal, the heroine always fell in love with them,' he told her grimly. 'And I'm not looking for a happy ending!'

Caitlin was breathing hard. 'That was fiction,

Rogan. Do I look as if I want a happy ending with you either?'

He shrugged. 'I'm not willing to take the risk.'

'You aren't taking me back because you think you've been selfish in bringing me here,' she accused. 'You're taking me back because you're *scared*, scared you just might find your emotions involved for a change. You——' She broke off as he quietly closed the door behind him as he left.

For the third time that day Caitlin began to cry.


She had fallen asleep!

It was the last thing she intended doing after the tears had subsided enough for her to think coherently. She was an O'Rourke, and the O'Rourkes fought for what they wanted. Against any odds.

But she had fallen asleep, when she had intended trying one last time to persuade Rogan they should stay on here a few more days!

She groaned tiredly, wondering at the reason for that tiredness. And then she realised it was still dark outside. What time was it, for goodness' sake? Three o'clock! In the morning, obviously.

She blinked tiredly, wondering what had woken her, listening to the wind blowing the rain against the window-pane. Rain? Yes, it was raining, quite heavily by the sound of it. She had always loved the rain as a child, and it was no different now. She was soothed by it for several minutes before she realised she really ought to go and investigate what had woken her.

Rogan had thoughtfully left the light on in the hallway, although his bedroom door was firmly closed. Perhaps he had thought she would try to rape him in his bed? Considering some of the wild schemes that had gone through her mind after he left her last night he hadn't been far wrong!

He had banked the fire perfectly, the continuing warmth in the cottage was proof of that, the dull glow in the fireplace looking as if it would easily last until morning. No, it certainly hadn't been the cold that had woken her. So what——

A high-pitched wail sounded at the back door, rather like a fretful baby.

Caitlin smiled as she guessed the identity of their nocturnal visitor, getting a saucer and filling it up with milk before opening the door to admit the cat.

He was a beautiful grey tabby with lovely white stocking feet, glancing at her curiously as he hesitated outside, his eyes unblinking, before he decided she looked harmless enough and walked inside to go over to the milk.

'You're a beauty, aren't you, Manxie,' she talked to him softly as she refilled the saucer. 'It's a little wet out there, isn't it?' She sat on the floor a few inches from where the unconcerned cat lapped at the milk. Wherever he had come from he didn't seem concerned by her presence so close to him. 'Would you like something better to eat now?' she offered, standing up carefully so as not to startle him before going to the refrigerator and cutting him some of the cooked chicken she and Rogan had bought that day. He tucked into it as if he hadn't already drunk two saucers of milk! 'You don't look as if you're starving,' she mused at the cat's nicely rounded body, receiving a glare from the green-gold eyes at her constant interruptions to his meal. 'All right,' she laughed softly, standing up. 'But there's a warm fire in the other room when you're finished here.'

'Caity?' Rogan called out worriedly. 'Caity?' he repeated softly, entering the kitchen. He frowned as he saw her standing there alone. 'I thought I heard voices?'

Caitlin was too affected by his appearance to answer him straight away. He was wearing a pair of pyjama bottoms resting low down on his hips, and what appeared to be nothing else, and his chest was a smooth bronze. His hair was rumpled, as if from sleep, although the grim expression in his eyes seemed to indicate he had had little of that the last couple of hours.

'Caity?' he prompted harshly. 'Who were you talking to when I came in?'

'Er—we have a visitor,' she informed him drily. 'Not that sort of visitor,' she added as he tensed watchfully. 'Manxie, say hello to Rogan.' She gave Rogan a rueful shrug as the cat continued to eat at her feet, quite unconcerned with the man who had entered the room.

'What the hell——!' Rogan moved so that he could see around the side of the kitchen unit that hid the cat standing beside her. 'A cat!' he realised disgustedly.

'I believe so,' she drawled.

He shot her an impatient look. 'But where did it come from?' He frowned down at the cat as if he had never seen one before.

'Outside,' she drawled.

'Caity——'

'Well, how would I know where he comes from?' she calmly interrupted his angry warning. 'I heard him crying outside the door, opened it, and Manxie just walked in as if he owned the place.'

'Manxie?' Rogan watched the cat as it finished off the last piece of the chicken.

'Because he's a Manx cat,' she sighed.

'I reali — my God,' his eyes widened as the cat put forward its front paws and stuck its bottom in the air in a satisfied stretch. 'It hasn't got a tail!' he told her in a panic. 'Do you think it's been involved in an accident?' he gasped.

'No.' She calmly shook her head.

'You don't think someone deliberately did that to a poor defenceless animal? I don't——'

'Rogan, I said he's a Manx cat,' she cut in softly.

'Even so, it doesn't—— Manx cat?' he queried as she still remained calm.

'They don't have tails. At least, some of them have small tails, but they're called—— Oh, look,' she sighed. 'I think you've offended him by talking about his lack of a tail; he wants to leave.' The cat stood at the door looking up at her expectantly. 'Off you go, then, boy.' She opened the door for the cat, watching as he ran off into the darkness.

'I've never seen anything like it,' Rogan spoke dazedly at her side. 'Now that I think about it I suppose I have heard about Manx cats having no tail, but—well, I've never actually seen one before. A cat somehow doesn't seem complete without its tail,' he frowned.

'The Manx are very proud of their cat.' She shut and relocked the door, reluctant to turn and face Rogan now that they were completely alone again.

'It's certainly unique.' He still seemed a little stunned.

'You should see them as kittens,' she chattered nervously. 'They're adorable. I wanted one when I was a child, but Daddy is a great one for leaving things to their own environment. And the island is such a beautiful place for them to roam free, much nicer than London. I don't suppose——'

'Caity.'

She swung her hair back down her spine as she raised her head to look at him. 'Yes?' Her voice was husky.

'What I said earlier——'

'I think you made yourself perfectly clear the first time around,' she assured him sharply.

'Maybe I was clear,' Rogan nodded. 'But I wasn't honest,' he rasped.

Caitlin tensed. 'No?'

'No,' he admitted. 'I still want you.'

Her first instinct was to tell him to go to hell, but then she realised what the admission had cost him. But that didn't alter the fact that although he still wanted her himself he intended taking her back to Graham.

'I think Manxie must live wild around here

somewhere,' she chatted lightly. 'My guess is that your friend Harry feeds him when he's here, and when Manxie saw the light he assumed it was him. He——'

'I was angry earlier,' Rogan cut in gruffly. 'Talking about my marriage has that effect,' he added ruefully.

'I only asked,' she defended, giving up all hope of avoiding the subject that had caused their argument earlier. 'There was no need to insult me.'

'I didn't mean to do that either.' He shrugged. 'I suddenly realised I was trying to play God with someone else's life when I've made such a mess of my own.'

'An unsuccessful marriage doesn't have to ruin your whole life!'

'Maybe not,' he acknowledged ruefully. 'But it does colour other events that happen in your life.'

'Other women?' Caitlin voiced quietly.

'Yes,' he scowled.

'And am I—like your wife?' She looked at him closely.

He gave a harsh laugh. 'I don't think anyone could be like my wife!'

That statement could have been taken two ways, and yet Caitlin was sure he wasn't still in love with his wife, which meant she had once hurt him very badly. 'Rogan——'

'I think we should both get back to bed,' he cut in abruptly, as if he regretted revealing even that much about his wife.

It could have been an invitation, but Caitlin knew that it wasn't.

'It will be morning in a couple of hours,' he added scowlingly.

And a few hours after that he intended disappearing from her life. If she had never met him she would have been married to Graham as planned, would have settled down to a life of complacency until one, or both of them had realised they wanted something different out of life. Or maybe they wouldn't, maybe if she had never met Rogan she and Graham could have made a success of their marriage.

But she *had* met Rogan, and she was a great believer in fate. The chances of their meeting at the hotel that night had been slight, Rogan's decision to come to London at that time at all, spontaneous. No, she believed they were *meant* to meet. If only *he* could be made to see that too.

'For God's sake get to bed, Caity,' Rogan rasped suddenly.

She looked at him with pained eyes, surprised at the harsh outburst. And then she saw the naked desire in his eyes and knew it was himself he was angry at, for wanting her as he did. 'Rogan.' His name was a husky plea on her lips.

A nerve pulsed in his rigidly clenched cheek, his breath released in a harsh hiss. 'All right, Caity,' he bit out tautly. 'If you want me in your bed tonight you're going to get me. I belatedly tried to do the honourable thing, but you've shot my control to pieces!'

She was pliant in his arms, loving the smooth warmth of his chest beneath her hands, the erotic movement of his mouth against hers, the faint rasp of his unshaven skin against her neck as he searched out the hollows of her ear.

Male nipples hardened beneath her touch, her hair brushing tantalisingly against his flesh as her tongue flicked lightly against the puckered nubs, his skin tasting slightly salty.

He drew in a ragged breath as her hands rested on the low waistband of his pyjama trousers, her own breath quickening as she realised how easily they could both be completely naked. And how she wanted that! She had never wanted a man the way she did Rogan, never felt this burning need to be held by him, *loved* by him. Even if it was only a physical love.

Her thighs were held firmly against his, telling her of Rogan's need to possess, and she arched up into him as his mouth moistly claimed one nipple through the sheer material of her nightgown, the gown clinging to her damply as he gave her other breast similar loving attention.

Their mouths fused together, bruising, hurting each other as they lost control to the searing ache, tongues entwined, searching, thrusting, *demanding*.

'Love me, Rogan,' she pleaded weakly against his lips. 'Oh, love me!'

Something in her words made him pull away from her. '*Make* love to you, you mean,' he rasped.

She blinked her confusion. 'It's the same thing,' she protested.

Desire faded from the dark green eyes, suspicion holding him aloof. 'Don't wrap up what we feel in a neat little *acceptable* parcel,' he bit out contemptuously. 'It's good old-fashioned want!'

'No.' She shook her head.

Rogan moved away from her completely. 'Maybe *you* have to have things all neat and acceptable,' he said coldly. 'But I don't lie about the way I feel, not even to get a woman into bed with me!'

Caitlin breathed in shakily. 'You don't love me.'

His mouth twisted. 'Don't fool yourself into thinking you love me either.'

'But——'

'Because you don't,' he stated scornfully. 'You want me, that's all. I knew it the moment we looked at each other. Then I thought we had plenty of time to pursue the attraction. I felt violent when I realised you intended marrying Graham, decided it wouldn't hurt if we had an affair first. Now I know differently.' He looked at her coldly. 'Go back to your bridegroom, Caity. Tell him how sorry you are for this attack of nerves. And then I'll come and dance at your wedding on Saturday!'

'You would still come?' she gasped. 'Even after— even after——'

'Of course I would come,' he drawled derisively. 'I'm sure you'll make a lovely bride—for Graham.'

The fantasy she had had of the two of *them* together crumbled before her eyes. Because she realised now that was all it had been, her fantasy.

Like the rest of her family she had fallen in love almost instantly, but unlike them she wasn't loved in return!

# CHAPTER NINE

THE island looked like a beautiful green paradise as the plane took off. Caitlin knew just how good it looked, because she watched it until it disappeared completely, and the plane was on its way to London.

She had got out of bed early, but it had been no hardship; she hadn't been able to go back to sleep after leaving Rogan last night.

It hadn't taken long at all to repack all her clothes, to feed the cat as he stood impatiently outside the door waiting to be let in. The seals were nowhere to be seen this morning, but after listening to the dawn chorus she had put some bread out for the birds.

One short day she had been back on the island, but she knew she was going to miss its natural beauty once she had gone.

She had been right! The plane had only just taken off, and already she wished she were back there. With Rogan.

It hadn't been easy getting a seat on the early morning scheduled flight back to London, but she had managed to get a last-minute cancellation. The taxi to the airport had been a litle easier to organise, and she had walked down the road to meet it so as not to alert Rogan to her departure. After last night they had nothing else to say to each other, and she

had no intention of letting him take her home like a
returned parcel he had decided not to open!
Because he had made his feelings perfectly clear; he
didn't love her and he never would.

And last night, more than anything else, had told
her how deep her love for him went.

She had been out with plenty of men, had found
most of them attractive—or she would never have
gone out with them—had even learnt to love
Graham, and yet never before had she wanted to
make love with any of them.

She was sure that was one thing Rogan *hadn't*
realised about her during his cold analysis of her
feelings. She, Caitlin O'Rourke, the sophisticate,
was still a virgin.

When she had started dating at sixteen it had
been fear of the unknown that held her back from
physical relationships. Her mother was a darling,
but when it came to anything of an intimate nature
she was more embarrassed about it than Caitlin
was. And the giggled boasts of her school friends
had done little to enhance the thought of physical
love; the whole thing had sounded degrading, and
not at all the beautiful act of love she had always
imagined.

After the fear had come the cynicism, as she
became old enough and wise enough to realise that
not all of those men were interested in her body
alone, that quite a number of them had their eye on
her father's money too. It quickly became easier,
and less painful, to shun physical advances with a
mocking laugh and an evasion of the subject.

But Graham hadn't tried to grope her on their first date, or worse than that, expected her just to hop into bed with him at the end of the evening. He had merely kissed her and thanked her for their date. Every date after that had ended in the same way, making it easy for her to respect and then love him, even to look forward with a quiet curiosity to their wedding-night.

But there was nothing even remotely quiet or curious about her feelings towards Rogan McCord.

Despite the way her mother and father, and then Brian and Beth, had fallen in love, she hadn't believed love at first, or even at second sight was something that would ever happen to her. She certainly hadn't expected love would come thundering into her life in the guise of a pirate with challenging green eyes!

What would Rogan feel when he found her gone? Probably relief, she realised ruefully.

At least this way she had saved him the bother of taking her back to London. He should thank her for that, at least, even if he did want to forget the whole ridiculous incident.

She didn't feel there was any need to burden her family with the complete fool she had been; she knew for a fact now what she had guessed at sixteen—that pirates were all rogues and scoundrels, and that they could never settle down with just one woman, that they didn't want to.

'Darling, where have you been?' her mother hugged her. 'We've been so worried!'

'I told you not to be,' chided Caitlin, smiling warmly. 'I'm sorry I just went off in that way. I——'

'It didn't matter, Caity,' her father assured her gruffly. 'Your mother and Beth dealt with all the details quite easily. And it was better you realise your mistake now than *after* the wedding,' he added ruefully.

'Oh, Daddy,' she walked gratefully into his open arms, 'I knew you would both understand.'

'And what about us?' Brian mocked as he and Beth came into the room, obviously having stayed on to help their mother. Beth was holding Matthew in her arms as he gurgled up at her. 'We had to be understanding too, you know. There was I, thinking I'd got rid of my little sister at last by marrying her off, and she changes her mind!' he added disgustedly.

'Brian!' his wife admonished. 'Caity could be upset about what happened.'

'I'm not.' Caitlin smiled at her friend. 'As for you,' she turned to her brother, 'you'll never get rid of me, married or not. I'd come back to haunt you from the grave!'

'Old maids seem to live for ever and ever,' he teased mockingly.

Her mouth quirked. 'That's because we don't have a husband to worry about!'

The family home had looked so endearingly familiar when she arrived home a short time ago that she had felt like crying, only the fact that it would seem strange when she had been the one to call off the wedding had stopped her. She knew her decison had been the right one, and the last thing she wanted was for her family to think she might be regretting it.

'Caity is far from being an old maid,' her mother defended indignantly.

'He only said that because he knows he robbed the cradle,' Caitlin taunted her brother.

'And after that disappearing act you pulled I expected you to come back with the sharpness of your tongue blunted,' Brian groaned ruefully.

She grinned. 'I may be down, brother dear, but I'm far from beaten!'

'I can see that,' he said admiringly. 'Why don't we all sit down and have some coffee?' he suggested lightly.

The ice had been broken with all her family, and she accepted the idea of coffee willingly, having left the cottage this morning without having so much as a drink, and having refused the offer of breakfast on board the plane.

Rogan was probably sitting down to a leisurely breakfast right now, grateful that he didn't have to return with her and possibly risk being found out. Maybe he would even stay on a few more days at the cottage, grateful for his lucky escape.

'—hasn't heard from him since,' Caitlin heard Brian say as she came back in on the conversation.

'Sorry?' she frowned when she realised he was talking to her. 'I was miles away.'

'I'd love to know where!' her brother said eagerly.

'Brian!' Beth gave him a warning punch on the

arm, glaring at him, although he refused to be cowed.

'I was just saying that Rogan McCord disapeared on Wednesday morning too,' Brian repeated softly, giving her a knowing look.

But he couldn't *know*! No one could know of that connection.

'Oh?' Caitlin managed to sound only mildly curious—thank God.

Brian nodded. 'He just left a note about some unexpected business that had come up, and left.'

'Really?' She gave her brother an angry glare for his persistence. 'Well, that was only yesterday, Brian.' Even if it did seem much longer!

'Mm,' he acknowledged. 'But I wondered if you happened to see him at the airport that morning. You never did tell us where you disappeared to.' He raised questioning brows.

'Is it important?' she asked sharply, her hands curved tightly about her cup. Brian had had a penchant for stirring up trouble ever since she could remember, and at the moment he was enjoying himself at her expense. He couldn't know anything, not definitely, but he was obviously having fun baiting her in this way.

'Depends where you went,' he drawled, shrugging.

'And who with,' the statement hung in the air but remained unsaid. To her parents the question must seem like a normal one to ask in the circumstances, but Caitlin was well aware of the speculation in Brian's eyes, could see by the sudden widening of

Beth's eyes that she had picked up on the implication too now.

'Does it matter?' she dismissed carelessly. 'I'm back now, and I really should go over and see Graham,' she added frowningly.

'Have your coffee first,' her mother insisted. 'And we don't really need to know where you went, just as long as you feel more settled now.'

Caitlin gave her a reassuring smile. 'I feel—I did the right thing.' She couldn't say she felt settled, because although she knew she had acted in the only way she could by calling off the wedding to Graham it was going to take her a long time to get over Rogan McCord. If she ever did. Surely that sort of love only came once in a lifetime?

'I'm sure you did.' Her father patted her hand. 'Graham is a fine man, but there was no point in marrying him if you didn't feel you could spend the rest of your life with him.'

'No,' she acknowledged sadly.

'So, where did you and Rogan McCord go?' Brian asked with relish as he sat on the side of her bed, having waited there for her to come out of the bathroom after changing.

Caitlin slowly entered the room, still brushing her hair. 'Mr McCord?' she feigned surprise, but she had known when Brian followed her to her bedroom after they had all drunk their coffee that he was far from satisfied with the explanation she had given downstairs. 'I hardly know the man.'

'I know.' Brian grinned his enjoyment. 'That's what makes it so much more interesting!'

She gave him a chilling look, sitting down in front of the mirror to re-apply her make-up. 'I don't know what you're talking about,' she scorned, studiously avoiding his eyes in the reflection.

'I'm talking about my little sister running off for the night with a complete stranger!'

Unwelcome colour darkened her cheeks. 'Have you taken to drinking alcohol for breakfast again?' she bit out cuttingly.

'Ouch!' Brian grimaced. 'Now I know I've struck a nerve; I know you like to tease me, but no matter how naughty I was in my wild youth you were never ever bitchy about it.'

She drew in a ragged breath. 'I'm sorry,' she sighed. 'But I have no idea why you persist in thinking I went anywhere with Mr McCord.'

'Because I know you, Caity,' her brother said softly. 'You took one look at Rogan McCord and decided you wanted him.'

'You make me sound like a spoilt little bitch,' she said irritably.

'You aren't spoilt.' Brian shook his head. 'You're just like the rest of the family, you know what you want, and you try to get it. And I wasn't fooled for a minute by that "mutual decision" story you and Graham told the other night!'

'It was the truth,' she flared. She had insisted on telling their families that in an effort to try and save Graham any embarrassment her decision could cause him. As far as Brian was concerned they could have saved themselves the trouble!

'If you say so,' shrugged Brian. 'But I also happen

to know of a certain assignation that took place between you and McCord after that.'

He couldn't possibly have seen Rogan leave her room that night! It had been a close thing, with her mother joining her seconds later, but she was sure Brian hadn't seen him.

'I'd got up to take Matthew to Beth for his early morning feed,' her brother continued. 'The two of you were very conspicuous sitting up on that hillside.'

He was talking about *yesterday morning*, Caitlin realised with relief. 'For your information, brother dear,' she turned to him confidently, 'I was on my way back to the house to go and meet Graham when Rogan and I met by chance.'

'You both happened to be up and out riding at six o'clock in the morning?' her brother scorned with disbelief.

'Why not?' she shrugged.

'Because it's too convenient, that's why not,' Brian insisted stubbornly.

'Daddy invited him to make use of his horse while he was here,' she informed him impatiently.

'And Rogan just happened to choose to go riding at the same time as you—before he did his disappearing act!' her brother derided.

'Exactly,' she nodded decisively.

Brian looked far from convinced. 'Where did *you* go yesterday?'

Caitlin stood up, preparing to leave. 'If you must know, the Isle of Man.'

'The Isle of Man?' he repeated, dumbfounded.

'But why on earth——'

'I can't talk any more now, Brian,' she told him dismissively. 'I called Graham as soon as I got up here and told him I would be over to see him within the hour. I have to leave now if I'm going to make it.'

Her brother sighed, still far from satisfied with her explanation. 'Don't worry, I'll get to the bottom of this,' he warned as she ran lightly down the stairs.

Knowing how persistent Brian could be, she knew he would try to do just that. But she wasn't going to tell him the truth, and with Rogan out of the picture there was no way he could find out what really happened yesterday.

Graham wasn't alone when Caitlin was shown into the lounge of his parents' home, Gayle was with him, but the other woman quickly excused herself, standing up to leave.

'You don't have to go, Gayle,' Graham grasped her arm, 'Caitlin and I don't have anything to say to each other that you can't hear.'

Gayle looked uncomfortably at Caitlin. 'I—I'd rather go. I—I'll see you once Caitlin has left.' She almost ran from the room.

Caitlin watched her go with a puzzled frown. Obviously it was difficult for all of them to be together when she had called off the wedding so suddenly, but the other woman actually seemed embarrassed in her company. She looked questioningly at Graham.

A dark flush coloured his cheeks. 'We have

nothing to be ashamed of, you did call off the wedding——'

'You mean you and Gayle . . .?'

'Why not?' he challenged.

'I wasn't criticising, Graham——'

'I should damn well hope not!' He moved to pour himself some whisky into a glass, taking a huge swallow. 'You cancelled our wedding only four days before it was supposed to take place, disappeared the next day without meeting me as we'd planned so that we could discuss if you still felt——'

'Graham, I *wasn't* criticising,' Caitlin repeated firmly. Although she was a little surprised; the two had never given any indication before that they were attracted to each other. Although who was she to question the suddenness of it when she had gone off with Rogan after knowing him only two days! 'Are the two of you in love?' she asked curiously.

He looked at her resentfully. 'Why should you care how we feel about each other?'

She moistened her lips. 'I just don't want you to make a mistake because of what I've done to you,' she told him gently. 'Two days ago you were happily going to marry me——'

'Until you decided you didn't love me after all!' he accused bitterly.

'It wasn't that——'

'No?' he scorned. 'Then what did I do that made you call off the wedding?'

'You didn't do anything.' She shook her head sadly. 'I'm very fond of you, I just—I just——'

'Don't love me,' he bit out. 'Well, Gayle does, and——'

'Graham, please don't ruin your life because you're angry with me,' Caitlin pleaded. 'If you love Gayle, that's fine, but don't do this just to get back at me.'

He glared at her angrily, breathing harshly, and then he sighed, dropping down into an armchair. 'I'm not being fair to you,' he groaned. 'I'm blaming you for everything when really we—we should never have been the ones getting married. I loved Gayle almost from the moment Thomas brought her home as his wife,' he admitted huskily. 'But she loved him, and I was determined to make a life for myself that didn't include her. Even when he died she was still his wife, and I thought I didn't stand a chance with her.'

Caitlin had sat down too now, stunned by what he was telling her; she had never realised he had such hidden depths to him. 'Go on,' she encouraged.

'I liked you from the first, I was sure we could have been happy together, but then the night of the dinner party Gayle was partnered with Rogan McCord!' His mouth was tight. 'Every time he made her laugh I felt like hitting him, and when he actually touched her ...!' Graham closed his eyes to shut out the memory. 'Then you called off our wedding, and Gayle had gone home with him, and by the time I got back here I was so angry I went straight to her bedroom and asked her what she thought she was doing with McCord when I was in

love with her! I don't know which of us was more
surprised when she admitted she was in love with
me too. I'm sorry, Caitlin, but I—I intend marrying
Gayle as soon as she'll agree to have me.'

'You mean you haven't asked her yet?'

He looked embarrassed. 'I didn't like to until I'd
spoken to you again.'

'And I did a disappearing act,' she realised
ruefully. She had to admit she was surprised to find
out that Graham and Gayle were in love; they had
both hidden their feelings for each other very well.
Maybe too well, which was why they hadn't
confessed their love for each other years ago! 'Well,
you can go and ask her now.' She stood up to leave.
'And don't forget to invite me to the wedding,' she
teased.

'That should really give the gossips something to
talk about!' he grimaced.

'Do any of us care?'

'I know I don't.' He stood up lightly, bending to
kiss her on the cheek. 'Thank you, Caitlin.'

'For jilting you?' she smiled.

He chuckled softly. 'Yes!'

God, what a mess it would all have been if her
marriage to Graham had actually taken place!
Graham and Gayle might never have actually
confessed their love for each other, but eventually
they would have realised how they felt.

Genuinely pleased for the other couple she
plastered a happy smile on her lips as she entered
the house. 'I have some wonderful news, everyone!'
she called out as she went into the lounge, her

breath becoming a strangled rasp as she looked straight into cold green eyes.

# CHAPTER TEN

'WE have a visitor, darling,' her mother announced unnecessarily.

'Yes,' Brian confirmed with the satisfaction of one who knows he is being proved more and more right by the minute. 'Mr McCord was able to conclude his business quickly and get back to us.'

Caitlin still stared at Rogan, the chilly condemnation in his eyes unmistakable.

'Yes,' he drawled as the silence lengthened out uncomfortably. 'I was just saying how pleased I was to be back in time for the wedding after all, but your father assured me there was no rush, that you and your fiancé cancelled the wedding on *Tuesday evening.*'

She closed her eyes at the accusation, wondering if she was the only one in the room to have caught his emphasis on the last two words. The only member of her family who seemed in the least curious about Rogan's attitude was Brian, and he was suspicious anyway.

Rogan must have left the island straight after her to have got here so quickly. She couldn't help wondering why he had gone to the trouble of following her. She hadn't expected it, had hoped that by the time he saw her father again her wedding, and the fact that it hadn't taken place, would be old history and so never come under discussion. *Why* was he here!

Her head went back challengingly. 'That's right,' she nodded abruptly.

'Am I to take it that your "good news" is that the wedding is back on again?' he said icily.

Her mouth tightened. 'No.'

'I'm sorry,' he drawled insincerely.

'Don't be,' she snapped. 'It was a mutual decision,' she stated for what had to be the tenth time.

'I believe you've just been to see your ex-fiancé?' he prompted softly.

'Yes.' Caitlin moved forward, breaking the tableau they made as they faced each other across the room, the rest of the family seated as they watched them with varying degrees of curiosity. 'I told you,' she dismissed, 'we parted friends.'

Which was more than they had done, the stormy look in his eyes seemed to accuse!

No, they hadn't parted friends, Rogan making his feelings concerning her perfectly obvious. Which meant he had no right to come here now acting as if she had done something wrong by leaving the way she had!

'I think everyone is longing to hear your "good news",' he drawled, sitting down, crossing one long leg over the other, casually dressed in black cords, a light green shirt, and a black jacket that stretched tautly across the width of his shoulders.

She shrugged. 'It really isn't that important,' she avoided. 'I'm sure we're all longing to hear about

the important business that took you away from us
so suddenly.' The moment she issued the challenge
she knew it had been a mistake; she could feel the
derision emanating from Rogan across the room.

'All of you?' he mocked.

'I know I am,' Brian said eagerly.

Rogan looked at the younger man questioningly,
his mouth tightening at what he read from his
expression. 'I'm afraid it was nothing very exciting,'
he drawled. 'Just something that didn't prove as
interesting as I thought it might.'

Caitlin paled at the insult, and would have told
Rogan just how 'interesting' she had found him if it
hadn't been for Brian's warning look. He was right,
in front of her parents wasn't the place to have this
out with Rogan.

'It would seem that we've both had a couple of
boring days,' she dismissed coolly.

His eyes flickered coldly. 'I'm sure a runaway
bride must be able to find something to amuse her,'
he bit out abruptly.

'Well, now that you mention it I did make a new
friend.' Blue eyes challenged green. 'His name was
Manxie,' she added with satisfaction as she saw
uncertainty flicker in those eyes.

'You mean you really did go to the Isle of Man?'
Brian frowned incredulously. 'Why on earth would
you choose to go there?'

'It's quiet. It's beautiful. Something just seemed
to take me there,' she shrugged.

Brian looked at Rogan thoughtfully, his expression questioning.

'Is lunch nearly ready?' Caitlin burst into speech. 'I didn't have time for breakfast this morning, so I'm famished!'

'You should always make time for breakfast, Caity,' drawled Rogan, letting her know that he at least had taken the time to enjoy some of the Canadian bacon they had purchased yesterday, before following her here. 'Lack of food is apt to make decision-making erratic.'

Her mouth tightened. 'My decisions are always perfectly lucid.'

'Always?' he drawled softly.

Colour darkened her cheeks as she knew he was talking of last night when she had asked him to make love to her. 'It's only when I make snap decisions about—things that my judgement is in error,' she returned challengingly. 'Then I'm invariably wrong.'

His mouth tightened. 'We all make errors of judgement we aren't too proud of,' he rasped. 'I made a serious one the last couple of days too.'

'Oh, I can't believe that, Rogan.' Her father's exclamation drew attention away from the fact that Caitlin had paled at the taunt. 'You're the most astute man I know.'

'Even I make my mistakes, Michael,' the other man grated.

He was interpreting her silence about her cancelled wedding in completely the wrong way, believed her to have been deliberately making a fool of him. And he was angry about it, so angry.

'I——'

'Why don't we all go in to lunch?' Brian suggested brightly, standing up to hold out his arm to Caitlin. 'Before our son and heir wakes up from his nap and prevents Beth and me from having ours in peace.'

Caitlin shot him a grateful smile as he escorted her into lunch, her father entering the dining-room with Beth on his arm. Rogan escorting their mother, remaining stony-faced as she chatted politely.

'I don't know what happened between the two of you the last couple of days,' murmured Brian as he held back her chair for her. 'But watch out for him, Caity; he's out for blood!'

She didn't need the warning; she could feel the resentment emanating from Rogan as they ate, and wisely stayed out of the conversation, although twice Rogan tried to draw her into it. He was obviously spoiling for a fight, but it certainly wasn't going to take place in front of her family!

'Would you care to go riding, Mr McCord?' she offered after the meal. 'As you saw the other day, my father has some excellent mounts in his stable.'

His teeth bared in the facsimile of a smile. 'I'd like that very much,' he nodded.

She hadn't doubted he would accept the invitation, had stood up even as she made the suggestion, giving him a coolly dismissive nod now. 'I'll meet you at the stables in ten minutes.'

'Fine,' he grated, his eyes cold as they insolently scanned the length of her.

Caitlin made as dignified an exit as possible in the circumstances, hurrying to her room once she was outside the dining-room.

'That was a wrong move, little sister,' Brian warned when he arrived at her bedroom a few minutes later. 'The mood Rogan McCord is in he'll rip you to pieces as soon as the two of you are alone.'

'Don't be ridiculous,' she dismissed irritably, very much afraid he was right; Rogan was obviously furious with her. 'And will you stop coming to my room with these wild accusations about him and me!' She tied her hair back, angry that her hands actually shook during the task.

'Caity, Mum and Dad might have been blind to the tension between their daughter and a supposed business associate of Dad's, but Beth and I weren't,' Brian told her gently.

'Beth?' She gave her brother a startled look. 'Does she realise how stupid I've been too?'

'Well, she insisted I come up here and help with Matthew and then told me to come in here and talk to you instead, so I would say she has a good idea,' he said drily. '*How* stupid have you been, Caity?'

She grimaced. 'Enough to make Rogan feel like wringing my neck,' she admitted heavily. 'If he comes back alone start digging up the grounds for me!'

'Caity.' Her brother halted her at the door. 'Remember,' he advised softly as she turned to look at him, 'he's only angry because no matter what you've done he still wants you.'

She wasn't so sure about that as the two of them left the stables in silence. She didn't look forward to the conversation that was about to take place, would much rather it had never needed to be said, but she knew it wasn't fair to her parents to avoid this confrontation and so increase the tension in the house.

She led the way, riding down to a stream that flowed about a mile away from the house, dismounting to let go of the reins, knowing Storm would only drink from the stream before nibbling at the grass. The two of them had come here dozens of times in the past, and he never attempted to run off.

Sitting down beneath the willow's draping branches had been a mistake, she realised, as Rogan towered over her like some avenging angel, his eyes glittering with cold contempt.

'So, Miss O'Rourke,' he finally bit out. 'All the time I thought I was trying to dissuade you from marrying Graham *he* had already decided he didn't want to marry you!'

'That isn't the way it happened.' Her eyes flashed. 'I told you——'

'I'm sure you had no choice but to accept his decision,' he scorned. 'Even to put a brave face on it.'

'Of course I had a choice,' she defended. 'He——'

'I doubt you could have forced him into marrying you,' Rogan sneered, dropping down on to the grass at her side, his fingers clasping her chin so that she had to look at him or cause herself considerable pain. 'Why didn't you tell me?' he rasped. 'Why go on with the charade?'

How could she tell the man who looked at her with such hate and disgust that she loved him!

'Well?' he demanded contemptuously. 'Could it be that the spoilt Caitlin O'Rourke was using me to bring Graham back to heel!'

'No!' she gasped her outrage.

'Then to salve your wounded pride by having an affair?' he scorned.

Caitlin wrenched away from him, uncaring of the pain she inflicted on herself. 'We didn't have an affair,' she reminded him heatedly.

'That certainly wasn't because of any lack of enticement on your part!'

'That was only because I——' She broke off, her mouth tight.

'Yes?' he prompted hardly. 'Because of what? My God, it all became so clear to me after your father told me the wedding had been cancelled!' He stood up restlessly. 'I found your lack of any real resistance yesterday morning puzzling at the time, now I realise that I gave you the perfect opening to escape what must have been a humiliating blow to you.'

'It was a mutual decision to call off the wedding,' she insisted heatedly.

'And how much was it influenced by the fact that Graham and Gayle want each other?'

Caitlin's eyes widened. 'You know about that?'

He shrugged. 'Only what I've seen,' he bit out. 'He seemed to be acting like a jealous lover when she sat with me the night of the dinner party. When I actually drove her home I thought he was going to hit me!'

Was she the only one who hadn't realised how

Graham and Gayle felt about each other?

'So he dumped you after we'd left, and you decided to salvage your pride by going away with me!' Rogan accused with disgust.

'No——'

'Or was it as I first suspected, you were hoping to bring him back in line by telling him of our affair?' His eyes glittered.

'No!' She gave a pained cry. 'I've told no one that I was with you yesterday.'

'Your brother certainly knows,' he insisted.

'Maybe because you remind him of what he once was, and he guessed how a selfish egotistical bastard would act!' she snapped. 'You saw something you wanted and you were determined to have it, no matter what the cost to anyone else involved! And now you're blaming me because your conscience reared its guilt-ridden head and you made the supreme sacrifice of not taking me! Isn't that really the reason you're so angry, because you found you had no need to resist me after all?'

'Damn you, Caity——'

'Do you want to take me now?' she scorned as he advanced threateningly towards her. 'Would that make you feel better?'

Rogan came to an abrupt halt. 'Maybe I don't want you any more.'

She knew that at the moment he did, but that it was an angry desire, one they would both view with disgust in a calmer frame of mind.

'Maybe I don't want you either,' she said dully.

'Maybe I don't give a damn!' His eyes were

narrowed on her flushed face. 'You still haven't told me which was the right reason, the need to salvage your pride or to get Graham back?'

'You seem to be the one who thinks he has all the right answers, why don't you work it out!'

'Caity!'

'It was neither,' she told him challengingly.

He looked at her consideringly for several seconds, his mouth twisting derisively. 'Then what was it?'

She would be taking a gamble if she told him of her love for him, but she had done nothing else since meeting this man, and she had nothing else to lose; he already despised her for what he *believed* to be her reasons.

She took a deep breath. 'I realised the night of the dinner party that I couldn't marry Graham feeling about you as I do. I couldn't make my vows to him when I wanted another man. The next day, when you took me to the island, I realised I hadn't gone along because I wanted to get away from all the gossip once the wedding was cancelled, that it was something else.' She met his wary gaze calmly. 'I love you, Rogan, and that's why I stayed on the island with you.'

If she had hit him he couldn't have looked more stunned. And then his eyes hardened, his mouth a tightly grim line of anger.

'What you *love*, Caity, is the thought of being married. And as long as the bridegroom isn't too disreputable you don't mind who he is as long as he can keep you in the manner to which you're accustomed!' he bit out scornfully.

'Surely that successfully eliminates you, then!' She hadn't meant to lose her temper with him again, but his contemptuous dismissal of her love wounded her deeply.

'I'm rich, Caity, and I'm sure all your friends would overlook my lack of the other social graces,' he said coldly.

'None of it's true,' she shook her head.

'Of course it is,' he rasped. 'And you aren't above being deceitful to get your own way either. But you made one serious error of judgement in your plans; I can't stand lies and deceit!'

'I didn't lie,' she insisted. 'I do love you, and I didn't tell you I'd already called off the wedding because if I had you—you——'

'Yes?' he demanded contemptuously. 'I would what?' he prompted softly.

Caitlin gave a pained frown. 'You would have taken your affair and then left,' she finished miserably.

'Exactly,' he said harshly. 'And you were holding out for marriage.'

'No!'

'Do you deny that you would have accepted if I'd asked you to marry me?' he taunted.

She swallowed hard, knowing how all this sounded to him by the cynical twist of his mouth. 'Marriage is a natural progression when you love someone,' she defended huskily.

'It's also quite convenient when one wealthy bridegroom backs out at the last minute!' he scorned. 'I'm only sorry I didn't come through with the proposal you wanted so that you could still have had your wedding on Saturday!' he added with sarcasm.

'I told you that isn't the way it happened,' she cried. 'Graham had every intention of going through with the wedding, I was the one who couldn't do it, because I realised I felt too strongly about you to marry anyone else!'

Rogan's mouth twisted. 'I've been married to one deceitful bitch, I have no intention of ever tying myself to another one!' He took the reins to swing himself up on the mare's back. 'I hope that's clear enough for you?'

She trembled at the disgust in his cold green eyes. 'Very,' she said shakily.

'Good,' he nodded grimly. 'Goodbye, Miss O'Rourke,' he added insultingly. 'I think I can contrive to come up with another business trip so that I'm gone from the house before you get back. I'll make sure that I do!' he rasped.

# CHAPTER ELEVEN

'YOU made a mess of things, Caity.' Brian shook his head. 'You should never have lost your temper with him like that.'

She hadn't come back to the house straight away; she knew Rogan meant it about leaving, and she couldn't bear to watch him go knowing he never intended to see her again, that he sincerely hoped he didn't! She had found him gone on her return; her brother was waiting in her bedroom for her, and she had just finished sobbing out the whole story to him. His conclusion came as no surprise to her.

'What was I supposed to do?' she sighed. 'Meekly stand there and take it while he insulted me?'

Amusement quirked Brian's lips as he looked at her flashing blue eyes and fiery-red hair. 'No, I don't suppose that is your style,' he drawled. 'But screaming at him certainly didn't get you anywhere, did it?'

'No,' she acknowledged dejectedly. 'But neither did telling him I'm in love with him.'

Brian frowned at this revelation. 'You didn't tell me you'd said that!'

'No,' she muttered, unable to look at her brother, her spine stiff as she stared out of the window. 'But why should I bother to hang on to my battered pride, it can't bring Rogan back.'

160

'He didn't believe you?' Brian looked at her closely.

'He told me I was in love with the idea of being married, not with him!'

'There's your answer, then,' her brother brightened, 'don't marry him.'

Caitlin's mouth twisted. 'I don't think I have any choice about that!'

'No, idiot,' Brian chided. 'I meant, have a relationship with him that doesn't involve marriage.'

She looked at him fully. 'An affair, you mean?'

'Why not?' he shrugged. 'He obviously still wants you.'

Caitlin wasn't so sure about that, but she didn't question the statement. 'You're very free and easy in telling me who I should have an affair with!' she said crossly.

'That's what big brothers are for,' he grinned.

'Really?' She raised her brows. 'I thought they were supposed to protect their little sisters.'

'You need my protection about as much as a spitting cat!' he dismissed. 'Besides, it sounds as if it's that or nothing with Rogan McCord.' He shrugged. 'I don't know why you're hesitating.'

'Because I—well, I——'

Brian looked stunned by the blush that coloured her cheeks. 'No,' he said slowly. 'You can't be!'

She gave him an irritated glare. 'Why can't I?' she attacked indignantly. 'Beth might be my best friend, but I'm sure once the two of you were married she told you that neither of us had,' she

defended herself resentfully. Anyone would think
she was abnormal, the way he was behaving!

'Yes, but that was three years ago,' Brian
dismissed, still staring at her disbelievingly.

'And now Beth is no longer a virgin,' she drawled
drily.

'But you are,' her brother realised softly.

'Yes,' she bit out. 'Don't get me wrong, I'm not
holding out for marriage, and if I thought it would
do any good I'd go to Rogan right now. But I think
he would feel my virginity was as much of a trap as
the love he refuses to believe is real.'

'Your virginity is very real,' Brian snorted.

'That's right, tell the whole household, why don't
you!' She glared at him.

'Well, I'm just so amazed,' he grimaced. 'You and
Graham never——'

'No, we *never*,' she snapped. 'And I can tell you
now that Rogan would just see it as another form of
entrapment if he discovered that fact now. He was
very badly hurt in his first marriage, and I came in
for the backlash of it!'

'I think I can understand the way he feels.'

'I told him you would,' Caitlin bit out. 'The two of
you are very alike.'

'We are?'

Brian looked as if she had just paid him the
greatest compliment. 'You like him,' she realised
with a resigned sigh.

'I think it's as well—as he's going to be your
lover,' Brian drawled.

'I told you——'

'I can't believe my sister is going to give up as easily as that.' He shook his head.

'I'm not giving up, Rogan won't allow me to get close to him!'

'You'll find a way, Caity,' Brian said with certainty. 'I'm sure of it.'

She gave a heavy sigh. 'I wish I had your confidence.'

'Sometimes we have to change to achieve what we want,' he told her softly.

Caitlin frowned. 'Like you did when you fell in love with Beth.'

'Exactly.' He stood up to squeeze her shoulder reassuringly. 'I know you'll find a way, Caity.'

But how? How could you force a man to want you? But Brian claimed there was no doubt that Rogan still wanted her. In normal circumstances an affair would have been the answer. If she hadn't been a virgin. Strange, she had never considered her virginity a burden before.

But did it have to be? She had read somewhere that today's women felt very little pain when they gave up their virginity, that the strenuous and active lives they led, and things like horseback and bike-riding meant there very often wasn't a barrier to break. And she had been horse-riding most of her life. And surely if there were pain she would be able to hide it from Rogan. It couldn't hurt that badly—could it?

Maybe she didn't have to change to be with Rogan, maybe she just had to practise a little of that conceit that he so despised but which was completely necessary in this case?

She had come to a decision, of sorts. Now she just had to see it through, or never see Rogan again.

'Daddy, I—er——' She had found him in his study, and stood uncertainly in the doorway. 'There was something I wanted to—to discuss with Mr McCord, and I—I wondered if you knew where he'd gone to?' The heated colour in her cheeks burnt her!

Compassion softened eyes as blue as her own. 'Darling, when Rogan left this morning he didn't give the impression he wanted to be followed.'

'But I——'

'Especially by you,' her father added gently. 'Come in and close the door, Caity,' he invited at her pained gasp. 'And let's talk.'

She went fully into the room, closing the door as he asked. 'I don't really feel in the mood for talking just now, Daddy,' she began.

'Not even about what happened between you and Rogan the last couple of days?' He arched one silver-grey brow.

Her mouth set angrily. 'Brian never could keep a secret——'

'He kept this one,' her father drawled at her fiery outburst.

'Then how—surely Rogan didn't tell you?' she gasped her disbelief.

'No one told me, Caity,' he assured her gently. 'I only had to see the two of you together to realise the attraction between you. And then when you called off your wedding to Graham and you both disappeared on the same day ...!'

'I suppose we were a bit obvious.' She sat down dejectedly on the sofa. 'So the whole family knows who I've been with since yesterday.'

'Not your mother,' her father smiled as he sat down next to her. 'She's still a little naïve about the determination of her children. But I'm the man who persuaded her to elope with me after we'd only known each other a week! I had a feeling both my children would fall in love as suddenly.'

'But you like Graham——'

'Of course I do,' he nodded. 'I'd be a fool not to like him. I'm sure you would have been happy with him. Not ecstatically happy the way your mother and I have been all these years, but happy nonetheless. Did he and Gayle sort out their feelings for each other, was that the good news you were going to tell us all earlier?'

'You know about that too?' she gasped.

'I may be getting on in years, Caity, but I'm not blind. I realised from the first that Gayle's feelings for Graham were far from platonic, but as he didn't seem to return the feelings I couldn't see it interfering with your relationship with him. Gayle would be far from the first person suffering from unrequited love.'

'I know,' Caitlin sighed.

Her father squeezed her hand. 'Are you sure your love for Rogan is unrequited?'

'Very,' she said flatly.

'Then why are you going after him?'

Her eyes widened. 'The man who has never

accepted the word no in his life asks me that?'

Her father smiled. 'I wish that were true, Caity, but sometimes I've had no choice *but* to accept it.'

She gave a pained frown. 'As you think I should with Rogan?'

'I don't know all the circumstances,' he shrugged. 'But I do know that when he left here a short time ago he wasn't a man who could be reasoned with. Maybe if you give him time . . .'

'I don't have time, Daddy,' she shook her head, 'he could be arranging to leave England right this moment.'

'He'll be back; we still haven't concluded our business,' her father assured her.

Caitlin stood up determinedly. 'What I have to say to him can't wait.'

'Sure?' Her father looked concerned.

'Very,' she nodded, giving him a rueful smile. 'Wish me luck?'

'I do,' he nodded, but he still looked worried. 'He told me that if I needed to contact him he would be staying at the same hotel as before,' he supplied.

To say Caitlin was nervous about facing Rogan again was an understatement; she was terrified. But she had come to a decision, and she intended seeing it through, no matter what the outcome.

Her nervousness wasn't helped by the fact that Rogan didn't answer the telephone in his suite when the receptionist insisted on calling to let him know she was here, rather than just telling Caitlin his room number as she had requested.

She turned away dejectedly, and then a thought occurred to her and she moved determinedly towards the bar where they had met that first night.

She saw him immediately, seated alone at the table near the bar, his expression grim and uninviting as he drank down what looked like whisky. She couldn't see the lovely Miranda in the bar tonight, but she doubted if she or any of her associates would dare approach Rogan in this mood!

But she had no choice, not if she wanted to talk to him, to be with him.

'Mind if I join you?'

He looked up at her with eyes as cold and uninviting as hers must have been that first evening. Was it only four days ago? She felt as if she had loved this man for ever.

'Please don't let me drive you away,' she added hurriedly as he seemed to be about to get up to leave. 'I wondered if you would be interested in buying me a drink?' she asked brightly as she sat down.

'Caity——'

' "Misery loves company", and all that,' she added lightly.

Rogan looked at her again. 'We can't start again, Caity,' he rasped as he guessed what she was trying to do. 'Too much has happened for that.'

She dropped the façade, and sat forward in her chair. 'What's happened?' she reasoned. 'My marriage to Graham is off—it doesn't matter who made the decison,' she added hastily. 'And so now you and I are both free to—to enjoy our relationship.'

'We don't have a relationship.'

'That's why I'm here.' She met his gaze steadily. 'You wanted an affair, so here I am.'

'You wanted to get married——'

'Not any more,' she cut in firmly. 'I'll take the affair you offered, because it's *you* I want.'

Rogan's eyes were like cold emeralds. 'Now?'

Caitlin had always found sweaty palms distasteful in a person, but she could feel her own dampen at the dispassionate way he discussed their going to bed together. But what else could she expect? 'Yes,' she answered huskily.

Rogan gave a cool inclination of his head, pushing back his chair as he stood up. 'Okay, let's go.'

Caitlin stood at his side. 'Go—where?'

'To my suite, of course.' He glanced at her. 'That's where the bed is.'

He was being deliberately insulting, and yet maybe he was allowed to be angry with her still. She *had* set out to trap him, but with love, never with artifice. If only she didn't feel she were about to make love with a stranger!

His suite was every bit as elegant and exclusive as the hotel notices claimed it was, but Caitlin spared her expensive surroundings no more than a cursory glance, following Rogan as he marched through to an adjoining room, coming to an abrupt halt as she realised it was his bedroom.

'The bathroom is through there.' He nodded in

the direction of a closed door to the left.

'I—er—I thought we could have a drink—or something, first.' She looked at him anxiously.

'Why?' he asked in a bored voice.

'Why not?' she snapped back. 'Rogan, do we have to—to jump straight into bed?' she added pleadingly.

He shrugged, his shoulders looking very broad in the dark sweater. 'I thought that was what you wanted.'

Tears filled her eyes. He couldn't mean them to make love so clinically! 'Rogan, do you have to be so nasty?' she choked. 'Coming here wasn't easy for me——'

'Then why did you do it?' he dismissed coldly.

Because she loved him more than she had thought it possible to love anyone! It was like a painful ache inside her all the time.

But instead of being defensive, as he expected, she attacked. 'I may have come here and offered myself to you, Rogan,' she bit out, 'but my name isn't Miranda, and I'm not a whore. Neither will I be treated as one! So if you——'

'I'm sorry,' he sighed suddenly. 'I was still angry about this afternoon, and I took that anger out on you. But I know damn well you aren't a whore,' he rasped. 'Let's go into the lounge and have that drink.'

Her breathing was shaky, her hand trembling slightly as she took the glass of sherry he had poured her and sipped at it gratefully. Rogan wasn't angry any more, but he was distant. And she—she was still terrified!

Neither of them seemed to know what to say as they sat opposite each other, and finally Caitlin was the one to speak. 'I think I'll take advantage of your offer of first use of the bathroom now.' She stood up jerkily. 'I—if that's all right with you?'

Rogan was watching her with narrowed eyes. 'You seem very nervous.'

As a new bride! 'I just want to please you,' she smiled shakily.

'Why should you doubt it?' he frowned.

'I don't—I just—we still aren't friends, not really.' She shrugged awkwardly. 'It seems a little—cold, to be going to bed together in the circumstances.'

'Caity, I'm not in the mood for sitting down and engaging in polite conversation,' he drawled.

Neither was she! Maybe the sooner the first time between them was over the better it would be, then they could start enjoying each other.

'I won't be long,' she promised.

'If you're too long I'll come and join you,' he murmured softly.

She hoped her escape to the bathroom didn't look too hasty!

The shower spray felt like needles on her flesh, and she felt invigorated and refreshed when she finally stepped out to dry herself, all the time terrified that Rogan would come in before she was dressed. It was then that she realised she couldn't possibly put her clothes back on, thankfully settling on the long towelling robe the hotel had provided on the back of the bathroom door.

Her breath caught in her throat when she emerged from the bathroom to find Rogan sprawled out on the bed, completely naked.

He stood up, brushing past her on his way into the adjoining room. 'I'll only be a few minutes,' he told her throatily, closing the door softly behind him.

She couldn't go through with this! It was too cold and unemotional. She loved Rogan, yes, but she realised now she couldn't belittle the emotion by taking physical love as a substitute for what she really wanted, and that was his love in return.

Her clothes were a crumpled bundle in her arms, and she tripped over herself as she tried to put them on before the shower water was turned off and Rogan came back into the bedroom.

She frantically looked around for something to write him a note on, finding a pad next to the telephone. 'I'm sorry,' she wrote. 'I love you,' she added when she realised he might read those two words and think she had been about to make a fool of him again and then changed her mind, then she quietly closed the door behind her as she left.

# CHAPTER TWELVE

CAITLIN touched the pretty lemon dress with gentle fingertips, imagining how she would look in it as she walked down the aisle later today.

Another wedding day.

And another bride.

Today Gayle and Graham were to be married, exactly a month to the day after Caitlin's own wedding to him should have taken place, and Gayle had asked her to be her bridesmaid. The last thing Caitlin felt like doing was attending a wedding, but she knew Gayle and Graham really wanted her to be there. And she also knew that quite a lot of people would see her reluctance to attend as a sign that she really did regret not being Graham's bride herself.

It wasn't in the least true, in fact she had helped Gayle with a lot of the arrangements. It had helped fill a lot of empty hours that would otherwise have been spent brooding about Rogan.

According to her father he had gone back to the States some time ago, and he had no idea when—or if—he was coming back to England.

It had been a long month for Caitlin, and even though she knew she had made the right decision at the time, she often regretted not stopping with

Rogan for that one night at least.

'Darling, that was Gayle on the telephone just now,' her mother came into her bedroom to tell her. 'She wondered if you could go over there now instead of later. Apparently the hairdresser made a mess of her hair and she wants you to help her re-do it. It probably looks fine as it is,' her mother added ruefully. 'But the bride never thinks she looks as nice as she can!'

There were still almost three hours to the wedding, but going over to help Gayle was better than sitting here until it was time for her to start getting ready. 'I may as well take my dress over with me now,' she decided. 'I probably won't have the time to come back for it.'

Considering it was October it was quite a warm day, and it wouldn't be too cold for the bride in her beautiful cream dress. Gayle had decided she couldn't very well wear white, but the cream creation she had chosen instead looked lovely on her.

Maybe—— What was that maniac in the car behind trying to do!

Caitlin hadn't been taking too much notice of the other traffic on the road this quiet Saturday morning—other than making sure she didn't hit anything—and she hadn't noticed the red BMW, or how long it had been behind her.

But she was noticing it now; she could hardly miss it when it was so close to her bumper!

The driver had brought the car dangerously close

to her, was going to cause an accident in a minute. If they didn't—God, what was the idiot doing now?

As she turned the corner the car levelled beside her, forcing her on to the side of the road.

After screeching the car to a halt she got out to march furiously over to give the driver of the other car a piece of her mind, the other car being parked behind her now. But the tirade never left her lips as she found herself staring into mocking green eyes.

'You could have killed us both just now!' she told Rogan breathlessly.

He leant his arm on the open window. 'A slight variation,' he drawled. 'But it will do. I don't think so,' he taunted in exactly the same way he had that day a month ago. 'From my vantage point I could see around the corner.'

'Your vantage point was the wrong side of the road.' This time the quote was completely accurate. 'Rogan, you look terrible.' She frowned at the loss of weight that didn't suit him at all, lines of tiredness beside his eyes and etched beside his mouth.

'Loss of appetite and lack of sleep will do it to you every time,' he said self-derisively.

'It must have been an important business deal.' Caitlin still couldn't get over the fact that he was here at all, let alone that they were conversing so naturally together. Where had he come from so unexpectedly?

'Why don't you get in?' he invited, indicating the seat next to him.

'I was just on my way to Graham's house.'

'I know.' His mouth tightened and the air of strain that surrounded him became more apparent. 'The two of you certainly believe in being unorthodox!'

Maybe being the bridesmaid at the wedding of the man she should have been the bride to the month before was a little unusual, but as she didn't mind she didn't see why anyone else should either. 'I suppose it is a little—unexpected,' she accepted thoughtfully. 'But as neither of us minds I don't see why anyone else should.'

'Get in the car, Caity,' Rogan rasped. 'I need to talk to you.'

She frowned at his sudden brusqueness. 'Rogan——'

'Please,' he bit out tautly.

Her eyes widened and then her frown deepened. 'What could we possibly have left to say to one another?'

'Get in the car and you'll find out,' he taunted.

Caitlin eyed him warily. She didn't understand what he was doing here, or why he had arrived so unexpectedly after a month of complete silence. But he was here, and nothing else really seemed to matter!

'Another hire car, Rogan?' She looked around the BMW as she moved to the side of the car to get in beside him. 'You certainly have expensive tastes. You—what do you think you're doing?' She had barely had time to close the door behind her before he put his foot down on the accelerator, shooting her back in the seat as he did so.

'Do up your seat-belt,' he instructed harshly, his expression grim.

'Rogan, I don't——'

'Would you like me to do it for you?' He gave her a brief glance.

She was too confused at the moment to withstand his touch without breaking down. 'That won't be necessary,' she told him haughtily. 'Rogan, wherever you're taking me I don't have the time for these games, I have to get to Graham's house. Maybe we can talk after the wedding if——'

'After the wedding will be too late,' he rasped.

Disappointment gave her a heavy feeling in her chest. 'This is just a fleeting visit, then?' She had been stupid to imagine it was anything else!

'No.'

'But——'

'Caity, I need to talk to you, but I don't intend doing so in a car going seventy miles an hour down the motorway!'

Motorway? They were heading towards London! 'Rogan, I really don't have the time for this,' she protested. 'The wedding——'

'You'll still make it—if you want to,' he added mysteriously.

'What do you——'

'You know, I don't remember you as being a chatterbox,' he told her drily.

Caitlin sat back in her seat in tight-lipped silence, hoping Gayle would manage to do her own hair, because it was a certainty she wasn't going to be able to help her with it!

She had already guessed their destination before Rogan parked the car in front of the hotel, following him inside and over to the lift to go up to his suite; if whatever he wanted to discuss couldn't be done in a car it certainly couldn't be done in a hotel reception area!

Once they reached his suite her unease increased with his obvious nervousness; it wasn't an emotion she would normally have associated with him.

He thrust his hands into the back pockets of his denims. 'That note you left here for me that night,' he looked at her fiercely, 'did you mean it?'

She blinked at the unexpectedness of the attack after a month of silence. 'That I was sorry? Of course I——'

'That you love me?' he cut in tersely.

She gave a pained frown. 'I'd already told you I did.'

'And now?' His eyes had narrowed to steely slits.

Caitlin drew in a ragged breath. 'I'm not as fickle as you'd like to believe I am,' she defended indignantly. 'I realise that my decision not to marry Graham was a sudden one, but falling in love with you was a little unexpected too!'

'Then why the hell are you going through with the wedding now?' Rogan demanded to know.

She gasped. 'But I——'

'I've spent the last month fighting my feelings for you, and telling myself I was wrong about you, only to find you've decided to go ahead with your society wedding after all!' he bit out disgustedly. 'How can you be so damned changeable?'

'I'm not—— What feelings have you for me?' she questioned as she realised what he had just said, hardly daring to breathe as she waited for his answer.

Rogan scowled darkly. 'I swore it would never happen to me again, was sure it wouldn't, but—I think I'm in love with you!'

'Think?' she croaked.

'All right, I *know* I'm in love with you!' he flared. 'A spoilt brat of a child who can't make her mind up who she wants to marry!'

She swallowed hard, her eyes wide. 'Marry?'

'Yes,' he attacked, standing so close to her his breath stirred the feathered fringe at her brow. 'And as you can't make the decision I'm making it for you; you're marrying me!'

'But——'

'No buts, Caity,' he growled. 'I'm going to make love to you until you're too weak to say anything else but yes!'

'Now?' she gasped as he clasped her hand in his much larger one.

'Of course now,' he pulled her in the direction of the bedroom. 'It wouldn't do any of us any good after you're married to Graham, now would it?' he scorned, throwing off his clothes.

'Rogan, about Graham——'

'Not now, Caity.' He tackled the buttons on her

blouse. 'Now is definitely not the time to discuss Graham Simond-Smith!'

Maybe now *wasn't* the time, she realised, groaning low in her throat as his mouth moved moistly over her bared breasts. Rogan was in no mood to talk coherently about anything at the moment, and she was rapidly joining him.

He was as beautiful completely naked as she had seen that night in this room a month ago, and after the other intimacies they had shared in the past she felt no shyness with him as he gazed his fill of her.

'You're so perfect, Caity,' he groaned, his eyes dark. 'So unforgettably perfect.'

'So it's just my body you're after,' she teased shakily.

'I want all of you, Caitlin O'Rourke,' he groaned. 'Even that cutting tongue of yours. *Especially* that cutting tongue!' His tongue engaged in a duel with hers as their mouths met in a fierce kiss. 'I love you, Caity. I love you so damn much!'

They were words she had thought never to hear from his lips, totally lost to the magic of his fierce lovemaking, as if he would stake his claim to her and her love by possession, unsure of any other way to convince her she was his.

He didn't remain in doubt for long; her response was unreserved, she was caressing him as he caressed her, feeling a burning need to commit every silken inch of him to memory.

There was only a brief moment of pain as his body merged with hers, and then she knew he was the other half of herself, the part that had been missing all her life, their bodies melded from breast to thigh in perfect harmony.

They moved together in unison, lips joined, hands touching, caressing, the fire inside them both burning to an aching spiral that threatened to demand release at any moment. They murmured words of love between kisses, words of encouragement, and finally of aching ecstasy as they reached that paradise together.

Caitlin had never known such contentment, such absolute fulfilment, snuggling against Rogan as he lay beside her, their bodies glistening damply.

'I guessed—I hoped—— My God, Caity, how could you think of giving that gift to any other man but me!' He held her fiercely against him.

'I didn't——'

'That night you came to me here and then left while I was still in the shower I half guessed it was because you hadn't been with a man before,' he breathed raggedly. 'You were so damned nervous, and you didn't seem to know what to do.'

'I do now,' she ran her hand lightly across his thighs, feeling his instant reaction.

'I don't mean in that way.' He halted the caress of her hand, entwining his fingers with hers.

'Oh, you mean I didn't know the right bedroom etiquette?' she teased, her eyes glowing.

'Stop being so damned provocative.' He tried to sound reproving but instead the rebuke came out as a caress. 'Why, Caity?'

'Because until you came along there was no one I wanted in that way.' She knew exactly what he was asking her.

'Not even Graham?' His eyes were narrowed.

'No,' she answered without hesitation. 'I don't find him repulsive obviously, but I don't ache for him the way I do you.'

'Then why——'

'Rogan, what made you think I was marrying Graham today?' He had sounded so positive she was, and that puzzled her.

His mouth tightened at the mere mention of it. 'Do you deny that the wedding is today?'

'No—but I wasn't the bride.' She moved to lean on her elbows at his sharply indrawn breath, looking down at him. 'You were right about Graham and Gayle, they do love each other; they're getting married today. I was just on my way over to the house to help Gayle with her hair when you stopped me,' she explained.

Rogan looked at her with searching eyes, groaning as he saw the complete candour in her expression. 'Damn them!' he rasped suddenly.

'Who?' She was totally bewildered.

'Your father and brother,' he scowled. '*Damn them!*' He sat up on the side of the bed, his face buried in his hands as his shoulders began to shake.

'Rogan!' She moved up on her knees behind him, tentatively touching his shoulders. 'Oh God, please don't cry,' she choked. 'It doesn't matter what they did, you don't have to marry me. You——'

He took his hands down from his face, turning to face her, not a tear in sight, his eyes brimming with laughter. 'Caity, of course I have to marry you; I love you.' He held her tightly in his arms, chuckling softly. 'It's my in-laws I'm going to have to watch out for!'

She was so relieved that he still wanted to marry her that whatever her father and Brian had done to persuade Rogan to confess his love she forgave them—later she would hug them both until they begged for mercy!

'I thought I was being so damned casual about it.' Rogan shook his head ruefully. 'A question here, a question there,' he pulled a face. 'And all the time they knew exactly what I was doing!'

'And what were you doing?' She kissed his shoulder.

'Trying to find out how you were without being too obvious; I guess I was obvious!'

'Not really,' she comforted. 'Both Daddy and Brian know I'm in love with you.' She kissed his throat.

'Caity, behave!' He put her firmly away from him. 'How could they have known that?' he frowned.

She shrugged. 'Because I told them. So what did they do to make you kidnap me again?'

He gave a rueful grimace. 'I was so determined not to feel anything for you that I went back to the States the day after you came to the hotel, was sure I could put you out of my mind. But the thought kept coming back to me that if you were the spoilt bitch I was trying to convince myself you were you wouldn't have changed your mind that night. It also occurred to me that you might have left because you loved me too much to belittle the emotion with an affair.'

She nodded. 'That was exactly how I felt.'

'After two weeks I came back to England, still fighting the way I felt, but desperate to know how you were, what you were doing. At first your father just casually mentioned that you were seeing Graham again. Then he told me he thought the two of you were arranging another wedding. And then this morning your brother had the gall to telephone me and invite me along!'

'That sounds like Brian,' she giggled. 'He always did like to stir things up—thank God!'

'Not just Brian,' Rogan said drily. 'Hearing that you were actually going to go through with marrying Graham I drove out to the house this morning determined to stop you in any way I could; your mother was the one to tell me you'd just left to drive over to Graham's house!'

Caitlin's eyes widened and then her brow cleared as she gave a glowing smile. 'Mummy and Daddy never have been able to keep secrets from each other.'

'And it seems I can't keep a secret from your family!' he grimaced. 'Once we're happily married perhaps they'll leave me alone.'

'Are you sure about getting married, Rogan?' She

voiced her lingering uncertainty. 'Your last marriage——'

'Was nothing like this one is going to be,' he stated firmly. 'And you are nothing like my ex-wife. I guessed when you left the way you did that night that you were a virgin; Pat wouldn't have hesitated to use that against me.'

'I was hoping you would never need to know,' Caitlin admitted with a sigh. 'That I would be able to hide the pain if only I could just be with you.'

'God, I never meant to make you ashamed of your virginity,' he groaned. 'Pat chose me as perfect husband material at the end of a long line of lovers. I was rich, went away on business a lot; I was perfect. I was fooled for about the first two months of our marriage, until I discovered the chauffeur she'd decided she needed to take her all over town to impress her friends, was also sharing her bed when I was away! She claimed it had only happened the once, that she was lonely when I had to go away on business, and so we decided to try again. Six months later one of my friends told me what no one else had the guts to do; Pat had been to bed with more than a dozen of our employees. When she came on to Greg he decided it was time to tell me what was going on. Of course Pat told a completely different version, but as Greg and I have been friends since high school . . .' Rogan drew in a ragged breath. 'She divorced me for every penny she could get her mercenary little hands on, and I let her. I just wanted her out of my life.'

Caitlin was very quiet after these revelations; she could see how he would be wary of her sudden change of heart about a moderately wealthy man in favour of a very rich one when he had already been stung so badly by one mercenary bitch. She hated Pat McCord for the mistrust she had given Rogan of all women.

'I told you, we don't have to get married.'

'And if my child is already setting up residence inside you?' he teased. 'Because I'm sure a little innocent like you isn't using birth control.'

She bristled angrily. 'Well, that's certainly no reason to get married! We——'

'We,' he echoed with satisfaction. 'You and I. Us. That's the way it's going to be, Caity. As husband and wife. Nothing less than marriage will satisfy the love I have inside me for you.'

She could see he meant it, that whatever doubts he had had about her in the past he now trusted her implicitly, that he always would.

'I don't remember being made love to until I was too weak to say anything else but yes,' she pouted.

'That will have to wait, wanton.' He pulled her to her feet, tapping her lightly on her bare bottom. 'We have a wedding to attend, remember. And I'm not going to be accused of making you miss this one too! We can do all our loving *after* we've seen Graham and Gayle safely married to each other. Then we can sit down with your parents and discuss *our* wedding.'

'I know a wonderful place for a honeymoon,' she

said throatily. 'Somewhere we can play our *own* games.'

'Harry has already accepted my offer to buy the cottage,' Rogan drawled.

'He has?' she said excitedly.

'He has,' he teased. 'Now about our wedding— you'll wear white, of course, as we've only preceded our vows by a few days at most. But *not* the dress you'd picked out to wear for Graham,' he added with a frown.

'Bossy, aren't you?' Caitlin said saucily as she began to dress.

'Incurably,' he confirmed unabashedly.

'You do realise my car has probably been stolen and re-sprayed green by now.' The grumble in her tone was belied by the happiness glowing in her eyes. She had never felt so happy!

'I'll buy you a new one,' Rogan promised indulgently.

'Keeping me in the life to which I'm accustomed?' she taunted cheekily, knowing that the painful things they had said to each other in the past couldn't just be ignored, or they would never be forgotten.

Rogan's hands linked at the base of her spine. 'The life you're going to become accustomed to is that of loving me, night and day,' he told her huskily.

She nuzzled her mouth against his. 'You're a rogue and a pirate!'

'You'd better believe it!'
She *knew* it.

**CAROLE MORTIMER**, one of our most popular—and prolific—English authors, began writing in the Harlequin Presents series in 1979. She now has more than forty top-selling romances to her credit and shows no signs whatever of running out of plot ideas. She writes strong traditional romances with a distinctly modern appeal, and her winning way with characters and romantic plot twists has earned her an enthusiastic audience worldwide.

## Books by Carole Mortimer

HARLEQUIN PRESENTS
804—CHERISH TOMORROW
812—A NO RISK AFFAIR
829—LOVERS IN THE AFTERNOON
852—THE DEVIL'S PRICE
860—LADY SURRENDER
877—KNIGHT'S POSSESSION
892—DARKNESS INTO LIGHT
909—NO LONGER A DREAM
923—THE WADE DYNASTY
939—GLASS SLIPPERS AND UNICORNS
955—HAWK'S PREY
989—VELVET PROMISE

HARLEQUIN SIGNATURE EDITION
GYPSY

Don't miss any of our special offers. Write to us at the following address for information on our newest releases.

Harlequin Reader Service
901 Fuhrmann Blvd., P.O. Box 1397, Buffalo, NY 14240
Canadian address: P.O. Box 603,
Fort Erie, Ont. L2A 5X3

## Can you keep a secret?

### You can keep this one plus 4 free novels

# Harlequin Presents

## Coming Next Month

### 1007 A DANGEROUS PASSION Jayne Bauling
Their meeting in Nepal brings instant attraction. Only later do their obsessions drive them apart—Grant's for mountain climbing, Renata's against climbing. How can they make a life together?

### 1008 STREET SONG Ann Charlton
Falling in love just isn't enough. Free-spirited musician Cara and a conservative businessman find their life-styles in no way mesh. Clearly something will have to change—but who and what?

### 1009 DANCING IN THE DARK Pippa Clarke
There's more to life than work. That's what a successful young journalist discovers when she falls in love with the paper's dynamic new reporter. But love and work sometimes get in each other's way....

### 1010 THE MARRIAGE DEAL Sara Craven
Reluctantly Ashley agrees the one man to save the family business is her ex-fiancé. Reluctantly she agrees to marry him. It certainly solves the company's problems, but creates personal ones when they fall in love!

### 1011 SUNSWEPT SUMMER Kathleen O'Brien
Interviewing newspaper magnate Rory Hammond in Palm Beach is a plum assignment, though Lucy takes it to get over the love they'd shared five years ago. Curiously getting mixed up with his current activities gives them a second chance at happiness.

### 1012 BEWARE OF MARRIED MEN Elizabeth Oldfield
Jorja likes her job in the Cheshire land agent's office yet she leaves when her boss declares his love for her. Past experience made her wary of married men—but the real trouble is she loves him, too!

### 1013 GIRL IN A GOLDEN BED Anne Weale
An English artist rents a villa in Portofino, Italy, and finds herself sharing the premises with the owner—a wealthy baronet! It's the summer of her dreams—until the lease expires, though not her love.

### 1014 CHALLENGE Sophie Weston
When Jessica's work throws her into the company of infamous playboy Leandro Volpi, he treats her like a battle to be won. And despite her talent for fending off unwanted overtures from men, Jessica finds Leandro a formidable opponent.

Available in August wherever paperback books are sold, or through Harlequin Reader Service:

In the U.S.
901 Fuhrmann Blvd.
P.O. Box 1397
Buffalo, N.Y. 14240-1397

In Canada
P.O. Box 603
Fort Erie, Ontario
L2A 5X3

In August
Harlequin celebrates

*The 1000th Presents*

# Passionate Relationship

by
**Penny Jordan**

Harlequin Presents,
still and always the No. 1 romance
series in the world!

# Janet Dailey

## Americana

A romantic tour of America with
Janet Dailey!

Enjoy two releases each month from this
collection of your favorite previously
published Janet Dailey titles, presented
alphabetically state by state.

Available NOW wherever paperback books
are sold.

# Sarah

## MAURA SEGER

Sarah wanted desperately to escape the clutches of her cruel father.
Philip needed a mother for his son, a mistress for his plantation.
It was a marriage of convenience.
Then it happened. The love they had tried to deny suddenly became a
blissful reality... only to be challenged by life's hardships and brutal
misfortunes.

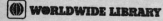

**For the millions who can't read
Give the Gift of Literacy**

One out of five adults in North America
cannot read or write well enough
to fill out a job application
or understand the directions on a bottle of medicine.

**You can change all this by joining the fight
against illiteracy.**

For more information write to:
Contact, Box 81826, Lincoln, Neb. 68501
In the United States, call toll free: 800-228-3225

**The only degree you need
is a degree of caring**